PEN PALS:
BOOK EIGHTEEN

DOUBLE DATE

by Sharon Dennis Wyeth

A YEARLING BOOK

Published by
Dell Publishing
a division of
Bantam Doubleday Dell Publishing Group, Inc.
666 Fifth Avenue
New York, New York 10103

ISBN: 0-440-40494-0

Illustrations by Wendy Wax
Published by arrangement with Parachute Press, Inc.
Printed in the United States of America
August 1991
10 9 8 7 6 5 4 3 2 1
OPM

To Kristie Dennis

CHAPTER ONE

———————⟨●⟩———————

Dark-haired Lisa McGreevy gazed wistfully out the window of her dorm room at the campus of the Alma Stephens School for Girls. The campus looked just the way she remembered it, but in the year she'd been away from boarding school, lots had changed. For one thing, this year Lisa would not be living in the four-person suite she'd once shared with her best friend Shanon Davis and their suitemates, Palmer Durand and Amy Ho. She would still be living in Fox Hall, but by herself—in a single.

Back home in Pennsylvania, the changes in Lisa's life had been even bigger. She'd returned home when her parents separated, wanting to be with them during their time of pain and uncertainty. But now that her mom and dad had finally made the decision to get a divorce and she was back at school in New Hampshire, Lisa wanted to put all of that unhappiness behind her. She could hardly wait to see her old school friends again—especially her pen pal Rob Williams, who went to the neighboring all-boys Ardsley Academy.

Turning toward the half-empty suitcase at the foot of

her bed, Lisa unpacked Rob's framed photograph. She had wrapped it in one of her sweaters so it wouldn't break. She stared fondly at the picture of her handsome brown-haired, blue-eyed pen pal, then placed it carefully on top of her dresser. At least one thing in her life hadn't changed, and that was her relationship with Rob. . . .

"Anybody home?" a voice called softly.

Lisa whirled around. A slim, sandy-haired girl with large hazel eyes was standing in the doorway.

"Shanon!" Lisa gasped, racing across the room.

"Lisa!" Shanon cried happily. "You *are* here! You're finally here!"

The two friends collided in a big hug. "I was looking for you everywhere," Shanon explained breathlessly. "I thought you'd be at Booth Hall registering."

"I was there," Lisa said, "but I guess we missed each other. Dad got me here kind of late, because he had to take my brother Reggie over to Ardsley first. . . ."

Lisa's voice trailed off, and Shanon gave her another quick hug.

"You're just the same," Lisa said, her dark eyes sparkling.

"You look the same, too," said Shanon, "only cooler."

Lisa grinned with pleasure. "Really?"

"You're wearing makeup, and you're a lot taller and . . . I like your air pumps," she added enthusiastically.

Lisa giggled and looked down at her shoes. "All the kids back home were into sneakers. I guess some of it rubbed off on me."

"How was it last year?" Shanon wanted to know. "You didn't say all that much about school in your letters. Was it fun taking classes with boys?"

"It was okay," Lisa admitted. "Some kids our age were

already dating. Of course, the boy *I* wanted to date was here in New Hampshire."

Shanon smiled knowingly. "You mean Rob."

"Who else?" Lisa said with a grin. "Guess what? When I was at Booth I checked my mailbox and I already got a letter from him!"

"A letter on the first day of school!" squealed Shanon. "Amazing!" She glanced at Rob's picture on the dresser, then looked around at the rest of the room. The walls were still bare and the bed was unmade, but knowing how Lisa liked to decorate, Shanon was sure that in no time at all the room would be beautiful. "Is your, uh, single okay?" she asked, shuffling her feet awkwardly.

"It's fine," Lisa replied quickly. "I know it wasn't your fault that we didn't get to room together."

"I don't know how it happened," Shanon blurted out anxiously. "We asked Maggie and Dan for that big suite on the fourth floor and we were so sure they would give it to us. But Renee Quick and Palmer's sister Georgette had put in for it first and—"

"Don't worry about it," Lisa interrupted, trying to be a good sport.

"But it would have been so perfect if you and Amy and Palmer and I and . . . Max could have lived together," Shanon continued.

At the mention of Shanon's new roommate, Lisa flushed. "Forget it," she said brusquely. "Besides, living by myself, I'll have more freedom. I can sleep late, go to bed whenever I want, keep the lights on—"

"Don't forget you're back at strict old Alma Stephens," Shanon giggled. "There are all these rules about lights-out and curfew."

Lisa groaned. "Ugh, I'd almost forgotten."

Shanon grabbed her friend's hand impulsively. "Come on. Let's go see Amy and Palmer. I hope Max is back from registration so you can finally get to meet her. I just know you two are going to love each other!"

As she dragged Lisa down the familiar hallway, Shanon called out, "Hey, everyone—Lisa's back!" Lisa grinned, both pleased and embarrassed, as a few girls poked their heads out of their rooms to greet her. She waved at upper-former Kate Majors and smiled at Muffin Talbot. But the real welcome came when Shanon threw open the door to Suite 3-D.

"McGreevy! McGreevy! You're back!" A short, athletic-looking girl holding a guitar bounced up off the pink loveseat. "You look great!" Amy Ho yelled, putting down the instrument to give Lisa an enthusiastic hug. "How are you doing?"

"Be careful, you're going to choke me," laughed Lisa, obviously pleased with Amy's warm welcome.

"Are you going out for soccer?" Amy asked, loosening her bear hold.

"I haven't thought about it yet," Lisa replied. "Are you?"

"Soccer's not my thing anymore," Amy said. "I'm saving myself for track."

"I see you're still into music, though," Lisa commented, glancing at her friend's guitar.

"What can I say?" Amy chuckled. "I'm a born rocker. Hey, Palmer," she yelled, "come on out! Lisa's here!"

"Is Max back yet?" Shanon asked, glancing toward the second bedroom.

Amy shrugged. "I think she's still at registration."

The door to Amy and Palmer's bedroom slowly opened and Palmer Durand sauntered out, a fashion magazine in her hand and a profusion of hot rollers in her hair.

"Hi, Lisa," she said, smiling sedately.

Lisa took one look at Palmer and a big grin spread across her face. Suite 3-D was just as she'd left it! "Hi, Palmer," Lisa said warmly. She looked around the room and sighed. "Wow! Everything is the same."

"The decor in Suite 3-D never changes," Palmer quipped, draping herself across the arm of a worn chair.

"I wouldn't change a thing," Lisa said, swallowing a sudden lump in her throat. "I like it. I mean . . . it's good to be back." She paused. "Feels kind of weird being a visitor here, though."

"The way they arrange the rooms around here is so dumb!" Amy sputtered indignantly. "If anybody should have gotten that big suite on the fourth floor, it should have been us."

"I told Lisa that we're really sorry about the way it worked out," Shanon said. "Poor Lisa, living by herself."

"I told you it's no problem," Lisa bluffed. If there was one thing she didn't want was her friends feeling sorry for her. "I don't want to be anyone's roommate."

"You don't?" Shanon asked in surprise.

"You know what I mean," said Lisa. "Since it worked out this way, I might as well—"

Lisa broke off in midsentence as the door to Suite 3-D flew open. A tall redhead wearing a red leather miniskirt, a New York Giants T-shirt, and a leather aviator's helmet walked in. Lisa knew right away that this had to be Max Schloss, the girl who had taken her place as Shanon's roommate.

"Hi, Maxie!" Shanon said, rushing over. "I want you to meet Lisa McGreevy!"

"Hi, Lisa," Max said in a friendly voice.

5

"Hi," Lisa said flatly.

There was a moment of uncomfortable silence.

"Max got a pen pal last year just like the rest of us," Shanon told Lisa, bringing up the one subject she knew her two friends had in common. "And Lisa's pen pal Rob has already written her a letter this year," she announced to Max.

"Rob wrote you a letter already?" Palmer exclaimed jealously. "That isn't fair!"

"What's unfair about it?" Lisa laughed, turning her back on Max and facing Palmer.

"I don't have a pen pal anymore," Palmer grumbled.

Amy giggled and strummed her guitar. "She's a lady who has lost at love," she sang teasingly. Palmer threw a pillow at her and Amy ducked. "Palmer's only had about a hundred pen pals in the last year and none of them worked out," Amy told Lisa, still giggling.

"No pen pal?" Lisa said sympathetically. "That's too bad."

"It's awful," wailed Palmer, examining her polished pink fingernails. "Amy has this guy Nikos Smith writing to her, Mars and Shanon are still writing, and Max has Paul Grant for her pen pal. But I have no one."

"Don't worry," Amy said. "If I know you, someone new will come along any minute now."

"You're probably right," said Palmer. "There must be loads of boys at Ardsley who'd like to write to me." She turned to Lisa. "So, aren't you going to read us Rob's letter?"

Lisa blushed. "I have it with me."

"Then read it," Amy urged.

"You know the rules," Shanon said with a smile. "Foxes share their pen pal letters."

"Maybe I'm not a Fox anymore, since I don't live in Suite 3-D," Lisa said, pulling Rob's letter out of her pocket.

Shanon winced. "Don't say that. You'll always be a Fox, no matter where you live."

Lisa glanced over at Max. Reading her private letter from Rob in front of a stranger made her slightly uncomfortable, but Lisa was eager to share the letter with her other three friends.

Lisa babe!

I am so glad that you are back at Alma this year! Check it out—the other good news is that I am on the football team. My schedule goes something like this: Monday: classes, football practice, classes. Tuesday: football practice, classes, football practice. Wednesday: football practice, football practice, classes. Anyway, you get the idea! Nikos Smith—your friend Amy's pen pal—is team captain, and he and Coach Ryan are running us into the ground. I can hardly walk, but it's worth it. As soon as I know my exact schedule I will write to you again so we can make some plans to see each other. Actually, I was thinking of sneaking into your dorm. So if you hear the window creaking open late one night, don't call the cops. It'll be me! My dad got me an electric razor and I'm giving myself razor cuts in order to save the money I would have spent at the barbershop. Ha, ha, my hair is kind of weird. When we do see each other, I hope you'll recognize me. Seriously, I cannot wait to see you.

Love,
Rob

"Not bad," Palmer said, passing Rob's letter around.

"Especially the part about climbing in your window. That's *so* romantic!"

"Definitely a cool letter," Max chimed in politely. "My pen pal Paul Grant is a good friend of Rob's," she told Lisa.

"I'm so glad Rob's on the football team with Nikos!" Amy exclaimed. "Nikos is the captain," she said proudly.

"What do you think, Shanon?" Lisa asked as Rob's letter nearly made full circle.

"From the very beginning there was nobody like you and Rob," Shanon said. "He's really crazy about you. I just hope he's not serious about sneaking into the dorm," she added nervously.

Lisa laughed. "He was only joking. But it definitely sounds like he missed me. I can't wait for our first date."

"Date?" Amy choked. "Aren't you forgetting something?"

"What?" Lisa asked.

"Alma Stephens is the same strict, boring place it always was," Palmer volunteered in response. "The only reason that I haven't got a boy in my life at the moment is because dating is nearly impossible. The number of times we can legally get together with boys can be counted on one hand."

Lisa giggled. "What about illegally?"

"You mean getting a pass and meeting in town?" Amy asked slyly. "That's always a possibility. But one of these days Dan and Maggie are going to figure out that when we write down 'studying at town library,' we really mean we're going for pizza at Figaro's."

"I don't know why they have to keep such strict tabs on us," Palmer said grumpily, "especially Dan. You'd think he was our father."

"Maybe that's because he *is* going to be a father!" Max chimed in good-naturedly. "Have you heard the great news?" she asked Lisa. "Dan and Maggie are having a baby!"

Lisa nodded. As freshmen, she and her roommates had watched the romance between Maggie Grayson, the French teacher and Fox Hall faculty resident, and Dan Griffith, their handsome English teacher, with great interest. It was hard to believe that in only two years the couple had married and were going to have a baby.

"I saw Maggie on my way to registration," Lisa said. "It looks as if she's going to have the baby any day now."

"She's so-o-o-o fat," Palmer said, rolling her eyes.

"It's all for a good cause," Max put in. "I love babies!"

"Maxie and I have volunteered to be baby-sitters," Shanon said brightly.

"We already take care of their dog, Gracie, together," Max added.

Lisa lowered her eyes. When she and Shanon had been roommates the two of them had also done lots of things together.

"Speaking of Maggie and Dan," Max said, "the Welcome Back tea is going to start in about five minutes."

"Five minutes!" Palmer exclaimed, jumping up. "I have to finish my hair."

"What's to finish?" Amy laughed. "Just take your curlers out."

"I guess I'll change into something less far out," Max said, heading for her bedroom.

Lisa winced. It had once been the bedroom she'd shared with Shanon.

"Come on, Shanon," Max called. "I want to show you the new stuff my mom got me. Some of it's a little conservative for me. Maybe you can wear it."

"Great," said Shanon. "Just a minute." She turned toward Lisa. "Want to meet us back here or downstairs at the tea?"

"I'm not going to the tea," Lisa said, getting up abruptly.

"You're going to pass up Maggie's brownies?" Amy said in shock.

"I don't feel like pigging out today," Lisa said. She headed toward the door. "Besides, teas are boring. I have too many other things to do."

"Like what?" asked Shanon, looking disappointed.

"Like decorating my new room and answering Rob's letter," Lisa said. "See you later."

As soon as Lisa was out the door, Shanon turned to the other girls. "I wonder why Lisa didn't want to go to Maggie and Dan's with us?" she murmured.

"She told us. She wants to write to Rob," Palmer said, breezing into the room, her blond hair looking perfectly—and casually—waved. "And I agree with her—teas *are* boring. I'm only going for the food."

"I just hope Lisa doesn't feel too left out because she's not living with us anymore," Shanon said, biting her lip.

Amy chuckled. "If Lisa doesn't go to the tea, it's because she doesn't want to. Lisa's rad. She always used to do what she wanted, no matter what anybody else thought. Why should she change?"

Walking out of the other bedroom, Max leaned silently against the door. So *that* was Lisa McGreevy.

CHAPTER TWO

"I can't believe how freaky this weather is," Palmer complained as she walked out of the gym with Amy, Max, Lisa, and Shanon. "I'm dying of the heat in this cashmere sweater."

"It's Indian summer," commented Amy.

"I need something cold to drink," Lisa announced. "Let's head for the snack bar."

"But Mrs. Butter is serving hoagies in the dining hall and lunch is in fifteen minutes," Max objected.

"So what?" said Lisa. She stopped short and Max almost bumped into her. "I hate hoagies," she muttered.

"Why should we spend money on lunch in the snack bar when we get it for free in the dining hall?" Max insisted, two pink spots appearing on her cheeks.

"Because we feel like it," Lisa replied, walking away. "There's no law that says we have to eat all our meals in the dining hall," she said firmly. "Isn't that right, Shanon?"

"Sure," Shanon replied, glancing guiltily at Max.

"How about you two?" Lisa called out to Amy and Palmer, who were standing a few feet away under a tree. "Want to cut over to the snack bar?"

"Sounds good to me," Palmer said. "I could use some nutrition after all those sit-ups Coach Barker forced us to do."

"Me, too," Amy sang out. "And on the way we can stop by the mailbox!"

The girls filed across the grassy quadrangle, with Max reluctantly bringing up the rear; but before they reached Booth Hall, she stopped short. "I'm going to the Music and Arts Building," she mumbled. "I have trombone practice."

"That's not until after lunch," Shanon reminded her.

"I—I need the extra time to warm up," Max stammered, heading in the opposite direction from the rest of the group. "See you later."

"Max really likes hoagies," Shanon said with a sigh. "Maybe we should have gone to the dining hall."

"Why should we do everything Max wants to do?" said Lisa.

"We don't do everything Max wants to do," Shanon said with a puzzled frown, "but she is a really neat person. Don't you think so?"

"How should I know?" Lisa said. "I just met her a few days ago."

"You're really going to like her," Shanon insisted. "Once you get to know her, the two of you are definitely going to be friends."

Lisa said nothing. With Amy and Palmer a few feet ahead, the girls walked on in silence.

"Are you sick or something?" Shanon ventured.

12

Lisa wrinkled her nose. "No. Do I look sick?"

"I was just wondering why you weren't in English class this morning," Shanon explained. "I thought you might be sick."

"I wasn't sick," said Lisa. "I didn't feel like going. I stayed in my room thinking about stuff."

"About your parents?" Shanon asked quietly. Shanon knew that her friend had been very upset by her parents' divorce, but since she'd been back at Alma, Lisa hadn't mentioned it once.

"Why should I be upset about my parents?" Lisa said impatiently. "If you want to know the truth, I don't even want to think about them. It's Rob that's been on my mind."

"How come?" said Shanon.

"Because I'm dying to see him," Lisa replied. "In person! It's so stupid that we're in the same state and we're still communicating by letters only!"

But when the girls got to Booth Hall, there was no mail in any of their boxes.

"A clear view of Ginger," Amy grumbled.

"What does that mean?" Lisa asked.

"Just something Amy made up," Palmer explained with a sigh. "You know Ginger is still the postmistress here. When we don't have any letters in our boxes, we can peek through into the mail room and see her."

Lisa looked through her empty box and spied the postmistress. "I see what you mean," she said with a feeble laugh. "Only instead of seeing Ginger, I wish I could see a letter from Rob."

"I'd like a letter, too," Palmer said grimly. "But of course without a pen pal, that's not very likely."

"Well, I *have* a pen pal," Lisa said impatiently, "but that doesn't do me much good."

"Rob *did* write to you on the very first day of school," Shanon reminded her.

"But I haven't seen him yet," Lisa said wistfully. "I have the feeling that he's so busy with football, I'll never get the chance."

"Don't despair!" Amy called out from the other side of the hall. "Look here! Ardsley is having a dance marathon."

"A dance marathon!" Palmer squealed, racing over to the bulletin board.

"For the benefit of the Ardsley Tutoring Project," Shanon read aloud from a large, brightly colored poster.

"Far out!" yelped Lisa. "Rob's going to love it!"

"Thank goodness it's not for another month," Palmer said cheerfully.

Lisa's face fell. "Another month?"

"Yes, isn't it great?" Palmer said. "That should give me more than enough time to meet the right boy to be my date."

"You don't need a date for this," Amy pointed out. "It's a benefit. They're going to be selling tickets."

"I wouldn't be caught dead at any dance without a date," Palmer insisted.

"I have a date," Lisa said, "but I don't think I can wait another whole month to see Rob. I want—"

"Good afternoon, girls," a man's bass voice boomed out.

"Hi, Mr. Griffith," Shanon replied.

"Hi," Amy chimed in with a grin.

Palmer batted her eyelashes at the handsome young English teacher. "Hi, Mr. Griffith," she said.

Dan Griffith flashed an easy smile. He had taught the girls for two years and had been their faculty dorm resident along with his wife Maggie for one of them.

"How are you, Miss McGreevy?" he asked, turning his deep green gaze on Lisa. "We haven't seen much of you."

"I've been having these terrible, burning migraine headaches," Lisa blurted out, blushing furiously.

"Too bad," Dan said sympathetically. "Is that why you weren't in class this morning?"

"That's the reason," Lisa replied, staring at her shoes.

"Migraine headaches are serious," Dan said with concern. "If you have another one, check in at the infirmary. And come down and say 'Hi' to Maggie and me," he added, continuing down the corridor. "We really missed you last year."

"Sometimes Dan can be such a pushover," Palmer whispered.

Lisa blinked. "I guess he believed me."

"If you had just told him that you were too tired to come to class, he probably would have understood," Shanon said.

"It was only a little white lie," Palmer chimed in. "Besides, if Lisa is going to skip class, she has to think of a good excuse, doesn't she?"

"Right," Lisa giggled nervously as the girls walked into the snack bar. "I can hardly tell Dan I was staring out the window, thinking about my boyfriend."

"I just can't believe that I don't even know any boys right now," Palmer groused on the way to the food counter. "I want you all to help me work out a plan of action over lunch."

"Are you going to advertise for another boy pen pal?"

15

Amy asked. She smiled fondly, thinking back to their freshman year when the original occupants of Suite 3-D had placed a "Boys Wanted!" ad in the Ardsley paper under the code name "Foxes of the Third Dimension."

"There's no time for that," said Palmer, peering at a selection of fruit. "I have to do something drastic. In three weeks, I have to meet a boy I really like and get him to like me enough to ask me to the Ardsley dance marathon."

"Sounds ambitious," Shanon said doubtfully. "Why don't you tell your friend Holbrook that you want to go?"

"Be real!" Palmer huffed.

"Who's Holbrook?" asked Lisa.

"A dweeb I met at summer camp," Palmer replied. "He happens to go to Ardsley, but I'm not dating him and that's final."

The girls set down their trays at their favorite center table. On one of the chairs was a copy of the Ardsley school newspaper.

"I can't believe it," Shanon said, picking up the paper and scanning the front page. "The first issue of *The Lion* is already out!" she exclaimed. "It's going to be weeks before Kate and I get the first issue of *The Ledger* to press. . . .

"Hey, look," she said, passing the paper to Lisa. "There's a picture of the football team."

"The football team!" Lisa said, snatching the paper. She drew in a breath. "There's Rob in the front row! Doesn't he look great?"

"Nikos doesn't look bad either," Amy said, peering at the picture over Lisa's shoulder.

"Let me see," Palmer demanded, pulling her chair closer. "Rob does look cute there," she complimented Lisa. "Nikos is okay, too," she added over her shoulder at Amy. "Of course he isn't my type."

Amy giggled. "Thank goodness."

"But if you ask me," Palmer continued, peering closely at the picture, "*this* is the cutest guy on the team." She pointed to a big, broad-shouldered boy with dark hair and an angular face.

The girls, including Shanon, drew in closer to get an even better look.

"Who is he?" Shanon asked.

"It says in the caption his name is Greg Proudfoot," Palmer reported. "It also says he's the quarterback!"

"Hey!" said Shanon. "Look who else is in the paper." She pointed to a small blurry picture at the bottom of the page. "It's your Holbrook Wellington," she said to Palmer. "He's been elected president of the Ardsley chess team."

Palmer gave the picture a quick glance. "He's not *my* Holbrook Wellington," she protested. "And he's even dweebier looking in that picture. But this Greg Proudfoot is great," she sighed, turning her attention back to the football team. "I think he's just the one to take me to the Ardsley dance."

"Except that you don't know him," Amy pointed out, downing her apple juice.

"A mere technicality," Palmer said slyly. She glanced at Lisa. "I know someone who knows someone who knows him."

"Mind if I keep this?" Lisa asked, picking up the newspaper.

"Why don't you tear out the picture and give me the rest," replied Shanon. "Kate's over at the *Ledger* office right now. I want to show her this issue. We've got to keep an eye on the competition."

Lisa carefully tore out the photograph while Palmer looked over her shoulder at it. Amy and Shanon finished their lunches.

"See you later," Shanon said, taking the rest of the paper. "I'll be at the *Ledger* office."

" 'Bye," said Palmer with a wave.

Amy got up and grabbed her knapsack. "Don't you two have history with me?" she asked Lisa and Palmer.

"I'll be a little late," Lisa mumbled. "I have something to do."

"Me, too," said Palmer.

"You know how strict Mr. Seganish can be," Amy warned, lifting an eyebrow.

"Lighten up," said Palmer. "We're not going to get kicked out of school just for being a few minutes late to history class. Right, Lisa?" she added with a bright smile.

"I guess not," Lisa said absentmindedly as Amy hurried off to class.

"I've got to figure out a way to see Rob," Lisa sighed when she and Palmer were alone at the table. Her eyes were fixed on the picture of Rob. "No matter what his schedule is, I have to see him." She tore a piece of paper out of her notebook. "If we were going to a co-ed school like I did last year, I would see him every day in class," she complained. "Without phones in our rooms, it's practically impossible to call him. Even if I stood on line for hours to use the pay phone, I probably wouldn't even get him. There's only one phone in Rob's dorm. It seems like the whole world's against us!"

"What are you going to do?" Palmer asked eagerly.

Lisa took in a breath. "I'm going to ask him out on a date."

Palmer whistled. "Heavy! I'm sure he'll say yes."

"I hope so," said Lisa, biting her pencil. "Where should I ask him to meet me?"

"Lulu's," Palmer suggested. "They have great music and the best food."

"Okay," said Lisa. "How about next Saturday?"

"Great!" Palmer exclaimed. "We'll get town passes. We can say we're going to the library."

"We?" said Lisa.

"Well, maybe I'll just drop by Lulu's, too," Palmer said blithely. "To check out what's happening. But you're the one who's going on the real date," she gushed. "And I'm sure that Rob will come. He definitely loves you."

Lisa sighed gratefully. "Thanks."

"You're welcome," said Palmer quickly. "By the way, while you're writing to Rob, will you do me a favor?"

"What's that?" asked Lisa innocently.

Palmer's blue eyes twinkled. "Just add a couple of lines about Greg Proudfoot . . ."

CHAPTER THREE

Dear Rob,

   I have been waiting for you to write me another letter. I really miss you! Could you please meet me at Lulu's this Saturday at twelve o'clock? No matter what, I will be there!

                               Yours truly,
                                 Lisa

P.S. I saw your picture in The Lion, *but since you were wearing your helmet, I couldn't see your new haircut.*
P.P.S. The Foxes saw Greg Proudfoot's picture in the paper, too. Palmer would like to know if Greg wants a pen pal.

Dear Lisa,

   I miss you a lot also. It has been so many months since we have actually seen each other. Last night I dreamt about you . . . again! To me you are like the person in the poem Shakespeare wrote—so beautiful that I could not even compare you to a summer's day. It feels like summer these days, doesn't it?

20

Man, do I sweat in football practice! My clothes are so sopping wet, you could wring them out. And when I get onto the scale I have usually lost at least seven pounds in perspiration! Hope you don't think it is too gross of me to tell you this, but I feel I can tell you anything.

To answer your question, YES. I will be at Lulu's no matter what! Anyway, I have asked Nikos Smith, the captain, and he said it could be arranged. What a great idea! You are very romantic, Lisa, and I like that.

Yours truly,
Rob

P.S. I asked Greg if he wanted a pen pal and he did not say anything. I think he was puzzled. He is a nice guy but not too talkative.

Dear Palmer,

Hi! It's me, Holbrook Wellington! I guess you're surprised that I'm writing to you. The reason is this—there is going to be a dance marathon at Ardsley and since I remember that you like to dance, I was wondering if you wanted to go with me. I am sure that lots of other boys will be asking you, so I thought I'd get my invitation in early, but I will understand if you say no. Write me back at your convenience. If I don't get an answer, I will assume that means you don't want to go with me.

Yours very truly,
Holbrook Wellington IV

P.S. We have an excellent library over here at Ardsley, as you know. I also have a computer in my room. So if you ever want me to do any research for you that you might not be able to do at the Alma library, please let me know. Also, if you have any math problems you would like help with (you said you hated math and most of your other subjects—I understand this, since not all of us are intellectual), just write to me and I will help you.

Dear Holbrook,

How nice of you to write to me. I saw your picture in The Lion! You are president of the chess team! Congrats! Thanks for the offer to help me with my math. But my roommate Amy is good at helping me and she's right here in the dorm. There is some research you could do for me, though. A friend of mine is interested in Greg Proudfoot. She thinks she might know him from some other time or place in her life. Maybe her parents know his parents. She isn't sure. Anyway, I would appreciate it if you could tell me anything you know about Greg, so I can tell my friend. That way she will know for sure if he is the person she thinks he is. Okay?

Love ya!
Palmer

P.S. Thank you for inviting me to the dance, but it is too early for me to say yes to an invitation, because I don't know what my plans will be. So maybe you'd better invite somebody else.

Dear Shanon,

I was late getting back to school this fall because the knee injury from my bicycle accident turned out to be more serious than the doc first thought it was. I am now working out at the gym to strengthen the muscles in my knee. Hopefully, I will be okay in time for the track team this spring. What's new with you? Have you heard about the dance marathon coming up here at the end of the month? I hope

22

you will be my date. (I'll try to dance on one foot!—just joking!) How are things in your suite this year? Did you girls get the big room you were after? Fill me in. Are you doing any extracurriculars this year? I am sure you are still writing for The Ledger. As for things back home this summer, everything is okay. My dad has another new job. I thought money might be a problem for my family again, but it looks like it won't be. How's everything at your house?

Write me—I miss you.

Love,
Mars (alias Arthur Martinez)

Dear Mars,

I was glad to get your letter. I am sorry that your leg is still bothering you. I am definitely writing for The Ledger, since this year I am the associate editor. Next year, when Kate graduates, I will probably be editor-in-chief. The big news here is that Lisa is back. I am so happy! She seems okay, but I think she is still bummed out about her parents. She doesn't want to talk about it, though, so I don't ask her.

Things got messed up with our suite assignment this year and Lisa was put in a single. I can't understand how Maggie and Dan could have done that. Speaking of Maggie, she is going to have her baby sometime in September. It's so exciting.

At my house, everything was okay also when I left. My sister Doreen decided not to go back to college and is in New York working as a secretary and going to fashion design school at night. Now the pressure is on me to get all A's (so far I've been lucky at this, but this year I've got

23

chemistry and I'm petrified). My dad is already talking about what college I'm going to! There is so much time to decide that, but it's all he talks about.

Mars, it is great having you to write to. I feel like I can tell you anything. Thank you for inviting me to the dance so far in advance. I'd love to come! I wish we could see each other before then, but I haven't heard of anything official I could invite you to here. Maybe we could get town passes on the same day and run into each other at Figaro's or Lulu's. By the way, I will be going in to Lulu's this Saturday with Lisa around lunchtime. Maybe you could come, too?

Take care of your leg.

> *Your friend always,*
> *Shanon*

Dear Maxie,

How are you? I am fine. I had a short vacation with my parents on our boat after camp this summer. It is good to be back at Ardsley, but the year is kind of slow for me. Something is missing. I guess I got used to spending time with you whenever I wanted to, like I did at Camp Emerald. I hope we keep writing this year. I am on the swimming team. How about you? How is your family? I hope someday to meet them. Write to tell me how your school year is starting.

> *Yours truly,*
> *Paul*

Dear Paul,

School is okay so far. I am on the swim team, too. My friend Amy, who is a jock in her own right, cannot under-

stand how I can bear jumping into cold water first thing in the morning. I am still living with Shanon Davis, my roommate from last year. But her old roommate, Lisa McGreevy, is back and I think Shanon would probably rather be living with her. My family is fine. I hope you meet them someday also. My dad is in New York these days, but his television series has been renewed, so he will be leaving pretty soon for California. This is very hard on my mother, who must stay in New York to work at her law firm. My three brothers are kind of wild and a handful. As for my other activities at Alma, I made the band. Paul, if you were me, and you believed deep in your heart that Shanon really wanted to be rooming with Lisa instead of me, would you volunteer to move out of Suite 3-D? The thought of it makes me feel awful. I really don't want to leave here, not only because of Shanon, but also because I like living with other people and Amy and I are good friends as well. But maybe it isn't fair of me to be Shanon's roommate when Shanon probably wants Lisa to be living in 3-D. What do you think about this?

Hope to see you soon.

Sincerely,
Max

P.S. I will be at Lulu's on Saturday at twelve o'clock if you are interested.

Dear Amy,

I'll be going into town this Saturday at noon. I am going to stop at Lulu's. If you are going to be in town, please stop by. How is your music? Are we still pen pals?

Nikos

Dear Nikos,

If you want to be pen pals, I want to be pen pals. My roommates are coming into town this Saturday, too, so I will definitely meet you at twelve o'clock.

My music is okay. I am in chorus this year, which is a different experience, singing classical-type things instead of rock. I still study with Professor Bernard ("Kringle"), who is strict but nice and looks just like Santa Claus!

I saw your picture in The Lion. *The team looks great! I can hardly believe that my pen pal is the captain. It must keep you really busy. Do you still have time for painting?*

Here is a song I'm working on. Let me know what you think.

Back to School Blues
by Amy Ho
Oh, it's back to the schoolbooks—
what a jolt to my brain
Let me hear some good rhythms—
to ease the pain
Double knot my red high-tops and
don't call me a fool
Getting ready for you babe
'cause you're all that is cool
But I'm back, but I'm back, but I'm back
But I'm back in school . . . get with it, get with it,
get with it, get with it. . . .

CHAPTER FOUR

—————⬧—————

"Have a good time," Maggie Grayson-Griffith called. The girls' faculty dorm resident and advisor waved at Shanon, Lisa, Amy, Palmer, and Max from the steps of Fox Hall. Wearing a stylish blue maternity shift and a light shawl, she was on her way out to walk her dog, Gracie.

"Anything we can get you at the drugstore?" Amy asked, pulling her bike off the rack.

"No thanks," Maggie replied. Bending down with difficulty, she attached Gracie's leash. "Dan's going into town himself today," she explained. "There are still so many things we need for the baby!" Maggie stood up and Gracie pulled at her leash. Together they started off across the lawn.

"See you later," Shanon said.

"Be sure you're back by four!" the teacher reminded them. "It may feel like summertime, but the days are getting shorter."

"Don't worry!" Shanon cried. "We'll be back before dark!"

The five Foxes climbed onto their bicycles. As Maggie

disappeared through the trees surrounding the quad, the girls headed toward the big iron gate at Alma's front entrance.

"We're free!" Palmer exclaimed. "Let's get over to Lulu's. Maybe Greg Proudfoot will be there."

"We told Maggie and Dan we were going shopping," Shanon said earnestly. "The least we should do is stop at the drugstore before we go to Lulu's."

"I don't need anything at the drugstore," Amy sang out.

"I do," said Max, "but I'll skip it, I guess . . . if nobody else is interested in going there."

"I have a date at Lulu's," Lisa announced. "I couldn't care less what we wrote down on our passes."

"Let's go to Lulu's then," Shanon gave in. "Actually, if Mars decides to show up, I wouldn't want to miss him."

The girls sailed through the gate with Amy and Palmer in the lead and Max, Lisa, and Shanon close behind them.

"Isn't it neat that Maggie and Dan are going to have a baby soon?" Shanon said, pedaling between Lisa and Max.

"I can't wait!" Max responded with a toothy smile. She glanced across at Lisa. "Isn't this weather great! What do you think?"

"About the weather or Maggie and Dan?" Lisa said, barely looking at her.

"Both," Max said enthusiastically.

"I don't have an opinion on either one of them," Lisa said, brushing Max off. "I've got other important things on my mind—like Rob."

Maxie's green eyes smarted. "See you later," she mumbled, pedaling faster. "I'm going to catch up with Amy."

Shanon and Lisa rode in silence for a moment. A clear, blue sky peeked through the yellow autumn leaves that lined the winding road into Brighton.

"This is just like the old days," Shanon said brightly. "Remember how the two of us went on that bike trip with Mr. Griffith our first year at Alma?"

"Huh?" said Lisa.

Leaning forward, Shanon craned to see Lisa's face. Her friend looked worried.

"Are you thinking about your date with Rob?" Shanon guessed.

"I'm kind of nervous," Lisa admitted. "It's been so long since I've seen him. Do I look all right?" she asked.

"You have on a lot of makeup," Shanon observed.

"Too much?" Lisa blurted out anxiously.

"Relax," Shanon encouraged. "It looks good on you. I'm surprised that Maggie didn't say something about your mascara, though."

"Why are you telling me this now?" Lisa moaned, leaning over her handlebars. "I need you to say I look great, not that I have on too much makeup!"

"You *do* look great," Shanon said apologetically. "I'm just not used to your wearing that much mascara," she continued, trying to explain herself. "Not that it doesn't look good on you," she babbled on nervously. "It's just different."

"I've been away from Alma for a whole year—I *am* different," Lisa said impatiently as the two girls pulled up in front of Lulu's.

Lulu's Diner, a local teen hangout, equipped with a jukebox, was located on the edge of Brighton's town limits. By the time Lisa and Shanon arrived, Amy, Max, and Palmer had already parked their bicycles next to some trees and were waiting to go inside.

"The joint looks like it's jumping," Amy greeted Lisa and Shanon. "I hope Nikos is here," she added. Pulling a

29

comb out of her back pocket, she ran it once through her black, windblown hair. "Now or never," she quipped, heading toward the door. "Hey, Max," she called back over her shoulder. "Check out the guy in the first window booth."

Max squinted and drew in a sharp breath. "Paul's here," she announced, catching sight of her blond pen pal's unmistakable profile. "I—I didn't expect him," she stammered.

"Don't be a goof," Palmer prodded. "Go inside."

"Isn't everybody else coming?" Max asked, hanging back shyly.

"In a minute," Lisa said. "I think I ate my lipstick off." She fiddled in her skirt pocket and pulled out a tube of Blazing Coral.

"I could use some of that, too," Palmer said, crowding in eagerly. "You can never tell who I might meet in Lulu's."

Standing by the bikes, Shanon waited patiently. Like Lisa, she had begun to feel a little nervous. Even though she'd been writing to Mars for two whole school years, it wasn't very often that she got to see him.

"How do I look?" Lisa asked, coming up to her.

"Terrific," Shanon replied. "Great! After that romantic letter Rob wrote to you, you have nothing to worry about," she said encouragingly.

Lisa have her a soulful look. "Sorry I snapped at you a while ago," she said. "Rob and I write great letters to each other, but . . . in person, it's different," she explained. "He means so much to me," she confided.

"Let's go," Palmer urged. "We've only got until four o'clock."

Smoothing her preppy-looking khaki cutoffs over her slim hips, Palmer marched to the door, followed by Lisa, Shanon, and Maxie. The diner was packed with boys and girls from Ardsley and Alma.

"Incredible," Lisa breathed, craning her neck to catch sight of Rob.

Shanon squeezed her friend's hand. "That's Nikos Smith," she said, pointing to a husky, curly-haired boy standing in front of the take-out counter. His arm was carelessly draped around Amy's shoulder and her hand was touching his waist.

"They look really tight," Lisa said enviously. "There are so many people in here I can't see Rob," she groaned.

"I don't see him either," Shanon admitted, peering into the crowd. "I wonder if Mars is here."

Lisa felt a hand brush across her back. "I've been waiting for you," a boy's deep voice murmured.

Lisa jerked around, startled. But the boy who had spoken wasn't Rob. He was tall and blond and was reaching for Maxie.

"Excuse me," he said, pulling Max forward.

Max stumbled and stepped on Lisa's toe. "Hi, Paul," she said shyly. "Sorry, Lisa," she added, finding a place for her feet. "This is my pen pal, Paul Grant."

"Hi," Lisa said, barely glancing at the boy. "Have you seen Rob Williams?"

Paul pointed across the room. "Over there," he shouted above the loud music.

Forgetting all about her friends, Lisa pushed through the crowd. Her heart was pounding as she searched for Rob. Squeezing past a circle of boys, she finally saw him pinned against the inside wall of a booth, resting his head in his

31

hands. A rowdy group of boys spilled into the narrow aisle between the booths and counter.

"The whole football team is here!" Palmer whispered, suddenly appearing at Lisa's shoulder. "That's Greg Proudfoot sitting next to Rob!" she hissed. "Get Rob to introduce me, okay?"

Lisa nodded absently, only half hearing Palmer. As she edged forward, her eyes were glued on Rob. He looked so pale, she thought. And his hair was kind of weird. The top was the familiar thatch of brown curls Lisa had always found so appealing, but the sides had been shaved almost bald. Rob's handsome face was still the same, though, and Lisa was incredibly happy to see him!

"Hi," she called out, stopping beside the booth.

Rob's blue eyes lit up. "Hi," he said. He struggled to stand up, but the big, broad-shouldered boy sitting next to him accidentally shoved him into his seat again. "Nikos brought the whole team over," Rob shouted over the heads of his group. "I guess we're kind of wild. Sorry."

Lisa shrugged and smiled. "That's okay," she yelled, trying to be heard.

"Any of you sweat hogs who haven't put in an order, get over here!" Nikos Smith barked from the take-out counter.

Half the boys at Rob's booth got up. The boy sitting next to Rob got up, to.

"Want anything, Williams?" he grunted.

"Later," Rob said, keeping his eyes on Lisa. "Uh . . . this is Greg Proudfoot," he added awkwardly. "You were asking about him."

"Hi," Lisa said, barely glancing at Greg's jet-black hair and chiseled profile.

Lisa felt a tapping on her back. It was Palmer. Pointing to Greg, she smiled eagerly.

"Oh—this is Palmer Durand," Lisa told Greg distractedly. As Greg wandered off to put in his order with Palmer not far behind, Rob slid over in the booth to make room for Lisa.

"How are you?" she asked, feeling a catch in her throat.

"Exhausted," Rob answered.

"Exhausted?"

"Fumble drill," Rob explained.

"What's that?" she asked, bewildered.

"A football drill," Rob replied. His hand grazed Lisa's fingers beneath the table and she felt her stomach lurch.

"Wow," she gulped, gazing into his eyes. "Here we are. . . . I don't know what to say. . . . Wow."

"Yeah, wow," he said, gazing back at her.

"Hey, Williams!" a boy roared from the take-out counter. "If you're going to chow down, you'd better put in an order!"

"Excuse me, Lisa," Rob said, standing up slowly. Lisa stood up, too, so that he could get out. "I'm really sore," he groaned, limping away from her.

"Sore?"

"Two-on-one," Rob muttered helplessly. "It's another football drill."

Lisa plopped back down into her seat. After Rob's letter, she had expected a romantic meeting at Lulu's—alone. She hadn't expected to be chaperoned by the whole football team. But maybe she and Rob would be able to step outside for a moment and go for a walk. Maybe they would hold hands or kiss. . . .

33

"Greg's even cuter in person," Palmer gushed, sliding in next to Lisa. "He's the Lions' star quarterback."

"That's nice," Lisa said, looking over Palmer's head. "Would you mind getting up?" she asked hastily. "Rob's coming back over."

"Gotcha," Palmer said with a wink.

Lisa's heart began to pound again as Rob limped toward the booth clutching a brown paper bag.

"Sorry that your muscles are sore," Lisa said sympathetically. "Maybe if we sat outside in the warm sun you'd feel better."

"Sounds amazing," Rob said, smiling weakly, "but I can't."

"What do you mean you can't?" Lisa asked.

"I've got to go now," Rob explained. "Football practice."

"I thought you just had practice," Lisa said.

"That was morning practice," Rob explained. "This afternoon the coach is going to—"

But before Rob could finish his explanation, Nikos Smith appeared. "We're out of here, Williams," he said, grabbing Rob's arm. "We've got just enough time to chow down, then it's back to the mines." He flashed Lisa a rueful smile. "Sorry, Lisa, but the team needs him. Once we whip this guy into shape, he's going to be dynamite."

Lisa sat dumbfounded as Nikos hustled Rob away. Just in front of the door, Nikos gave Amy a hug. "Sorry," Rob called out in Lisa's direction. "I . . . I'll be in touch!"

Suddenly the tiny restaurant was almost quiet. At least ten of the noisiest customers had disappeared with the football team. Shanon, Palmer, and Amy crossed to Lisa's booth, carrying soft drinks.

34

"Mars didn't come," Shanon reported in a disappointed voice. "Want some?" she asked, sliding her Coke over to Lisa.

Lisa took a sip without answering. At the moment she couldn't think about Shanon. She had problems of her own.

"I saw you talking with Rob over here," Amy said, jabbing Lisa's arm playfully. "Nikos says he's a real asset to the team."

Lisa took another sip of Shanon's Coke and glared at Amy. If it hadn't been for Nikos, she thought, Rob might still be there.

"You and Max and Amy are so lucky!" Palmer exclaimed. "You got to see Rob, Amy got to see Nikos, and look at Max!" She pointed to the corner booth. "She and Paul are still over there."

Lisa darted a glance in Max's direction. Sitting across from each other at their own little booth, she and Paul Grant were laughing carelessly. They looked so happy together, just the way Lisa had imagined her own date with Rob. Seeing Max with Paul made Lisa more jealous than ever of Shanon's new roommate.

"Things seem to be warming up between Max and Paul," Palmer observed.

"I'm so glad," Shanon said. "When she gets around boys, Max can sometimes be shy."

"Will you stop talking about Max and her boyfriend?" Lisa exploded. "Furthermore," she announced, "I am *not* lucky. This has been the most horrible afternoon of my life and I'm going home!"

"To Pennsylvania?" Shanon asked in surprise.

"Of course not," Lisa said, getting up suddenly. "I'm

going to school, to my room." Blinking back tears of anger and frustration, she scrambled over Shanon and bolted out of the booth.

"Poor Lisa," Shanon said quietly.

"And don't *Poor Lisa* me, either!" Lisa cried. "Just . . . just leave me alone!"

Shanon watched helplessly as Lisa pushed through the door of the diner.

Outside, Lisa took a big gulp of fresh air. *Rob doesn't really love me!* she thought. Jumping onto her bike, she pedaled furiously. If Rob loved her, he would have stayed! He would have told Nikos that his date with her was more important than any stupid football practice!

Lisa arrived back at Alma in record time, angry and winded. Dashing up the stairs past Maggie, she headed straight for her room.

"Is anything wrong?" Maggie called out in concern.

"No!" Lisa shouted down tersely, then slammed her door.

For once she was glad she lived in a single. It was bad enough being humiliated by the one boy in the world she thought she could count on—at least she didn't have to face a suite full of girls saying "Poor Lisa!" Reaching down toward the pile of books on the floor, she grabbed a pad of paper and started to write.

Dear Rob,
  If you want to know what I think of our date at Lulu's, I hated it!

                                                             Love,
                                                             Lisa

P.S. Your haircut stinks!!

CHAPTER FIVE

"Lisa!" Shanon hissed. "Wake up!" The two girls were sitting in the second row of the auditorium, right in the line of Miss Pryn's vision. At one point, it seemed to Shanon that the headmistress had actually glared at them.

"Miss Pryn's looking at you," Shanon whispered out of the side of her mouth.

Lisa opened one eye. "I'm not sleeping," she grunted.

Fortunately, at that moment Miss Pryn sat down and the meeting was taken over by the Council president, Brenda Smith.

"Let's get out of here," Lisa suggested, elbowing Shanon.

Reddening in embarrassment, Shanon followed Lisa out of the room.

"The meeting was almost over," she complained once they were outside the auditorium.

"The better to leave now and avoid the crowds, my dear!" Lisa quipped. She put her red baseball cap on backward and stuck her tongue out at the door. "That's what I think of that boring old Student Council," she said with a chuckle. "Haven't they got anything better to do than listen to boring old Miss Pryn all day?"

Shanon shook her head in frustration. It seemed to her that Lisa's attitude was getting worse and worse. "You're lucky Miss Pryn didn't say anything about your skirt," Shanon said as they pushed through the front door and out onto the quad.

"So what if she did?" Lisa replied, hitching up her bright blue miniskirt.

"You know how strict the dress code is here," Shanon warned. "Yesterday you wore pants to Mr. Griffith's class."

Lisa rolled her eyes. "Well, Dan didn't say anything about it. Guess he was more upset because I forgot my English homework."

"You didn't even *do* it," Shanon said quietly. "I know because Palmer told me you didn't. She said that the two of you were in your room and you decided to play cards instead."

Lisa turned abruptly and stared. "Will you give me a break?" she said. "You've been telling me what to do ever since I came back, as if I don't know the difference between right and wrong. You're worse than my mother."

"And ever since you came back, you've been putting me down and hurting my feelings!" Shanon blurted out.

"I have?" Lisa said, startled by the pained expression on Shanon's face. "How have I hurt your feelings?" she asked.

"You're always snapping at me," Shanon sputtered. "And every time Max is around, you give her the cold shoulder! And there are other people whose feelings you've hurt, too!" she continued stubbornly.

"Like whose?" Lisa challenged, putting her hands on her

hips. "If anyone should have hurt feelings, it's me! I'm the one who got kicked out of Suite 3-D! I'm the one whose parents got divorced! I'm the one whose boyfriend doesn't care anything about her anymore!"

Shanon grabbed Lisa's arm. "Come upstairs," she directed. "I have something to show you." The two girls marched back to 3-D in silence.

The suite was empty. Lisa followed Shanon into her room. Once it had been her room, too, thought Lisa sadly; now Shanon shared it with Maxie.

"I don't think I've been in your room more than a couple of times this year," Lisa said, perching on the foot of Max's bed. "Whenever I come over, we hang out mostly in the sitting room. I like this bedspread," she commented, fingering the Indian print on Max's bed. "Remember the matching quilts your mom got us when we lived here together?"

"I remember," Shanon said quietly. She crossed to the desk in the corner. "This is what I wanted to show you," she said, taking an envelope out of the drawer. "Mars wrote to me."

"Great!" said Lisa.

"I think you'd better read it first," said Shanon.

Lisa picked up the letter.

Dear Shanon,

I stood you up at Lulu's! That's because I couldn't stand up anywhere. My knee gave out on me and the nurse at the infirmary had to take me in to the hospital! I may have to have another operation. But never fear, your Mars will survive for the big dance marathon. I'm working on a

*break dance (get it—break?) that's out of sight. Anyway,
please forgive me for standing you up. . . .*

"Wow, that's too bad," Lisa murmured. "No wonder
you're so bummed out this morning. Poor Mars."

"Read the next part," Shanon said.

*There's another mission I have in writing to you today.
I am making a plea on behalf of my buddy Rob Williams.
Will you please ask Lisa McGreevy to lay off the guy. Rob
is being pushed to his limits on the team this year. Football
has always been his dream, but he is also totally out of his
mind in love with Lisa. And what did your friend do to
Rob? She sent him a "hate" letter. Williams never was the
type to emote a lot, but now he's so bummed out, he's
practically stopped talking. Not only did Lisa say that she
hated their date, but she also has given him an inferiority
complex about his new haircut. Soon the poor guy will be
wearing a football helmet in the shower. Seriously, Rob is
in bad shape—he is sure that Lisa is going to dump him.
Please ask your friend to give my friend a break! (Not a
break in the knee like I have! Oh, what a joker I am! Just
beg Lisa not to break this guy's heart!)*

Catch you later, alligator!
Your ever lovin' Arthur "Mars" Martinez

"Oh, no," Lisa groaned. Collapsing onto Maxie's bed,
she laid the letter on her face. "What am I going to do
now?" she wailed.

"Patch it up with Rob," Shanon said kindly. "Don't you
see? If he's so upset about the letter you sent him, he must
really love you."

40

"I guess he does," Lisa said with a hopeful gleam in her eyes. "I shouldn't have sent him that mean letter. My feelings were so hurt, though, when he left Lulu's right after I came in, just because the football team was going."

"If he could have stayed longer, I'm sure he would have," Shanon reasoned. "He was probably just as disappointed as you were with your date. Now, from what Mars says in his letter, Rob is worried that you don't like him anymore."

"But I do!" Lisa exclaimed. "I more than like him! All the while I was having that horrible time with Mom and Dad last year and Rob was writing to me, I kept telling myself that I shouldn't be unhappy because, no matter what, I could count on Rob. He would always love me and never change! I guess I was expecting something unbelievable to happen the first time I saw him again," she said sheepishly. "When he had to leave right away, I was afraid that he *had* changed . . . that he didn't love me anymore."

"But now you see he hasn't changed," said Shanon. She blushed slightly. "I, uh, haven't changed either, you know. I still think of you as my best friend."

"You do?" said Lisa. "Even though we're not roommates?"

"Just because we don't live together doesn't mean we can't be best friends," said Shanon.

Lisa glanced around the room. "I was really upset when I didn't get into the suite again."

"I thought you said you didn't want a roommate," said Shanon.

"I only said that because I didn't want everybody feeling sorry for me," Lisa confessed.

"I wish we could change things," said Shanon.

Lisa shrugged. "Actually, it's not so bad being in a single. I can sleep late, keep the light on at night, even skip class," she said with a chuckle.

"You've been doing that a lot," Shanon said, giving her friend a worried look. "I hope you don't get into trouble."

Lisa smiled. "I'm not going to get kicked out of school for missing class a couple of times," she said confidently. "You've gotten too used to it around here, so you're scared of the rules. At the school I went to last year," she continued eagerly, "there weren't any rules. That's one part of it I liked—believe me!"

"No rules?" Shanon said wide-eyed.

"Well, some. But not nearly as many as there are here," Lisa said. "You could dress the way you want, wear makeup. If you missed class every once in a while, you might get called in to see the principal. But there wasn't any of this demerit stuff like Alma has. The best thing," she added, "was that I could come and go as I pleased. I didn't have to ask permission to go to the drugstore for a hair clip."

"Didn't your mom and dad have anything to say about where you went?" Shanon asked.

A shadow passed over Lisa's face. "They were so wrapped up in their own problems, I don't think they noticed," she mumbled. "So I got to have fun!" she added, forcing a smile.

"I'm sorry if I've been hurting your feelings," she said, crossing over to Shanon. "You are absolutely my best friend."

"I wish you could get to like Max, too," Shanon sighed.

Lisa looked skeptical.

"She's so nice," Shanon insisted. "And it's not her fault that she's my roommate. Could you try to be a little nicer to her?"

Lisa lowered her eyes. She knew Shanon was right. She had been snubbing Max because she was jealous. "I'll try," she promised. Snatching up her hat, she marched to the door. "I'm so glad to know that Rob still loves me!" she said. "Now I have to go write him a nice juicy letter. Poor guy—I hope he doesn't really try showering with his football helmet on!"

As Lisa was leaving the room, Max came in.

"Hi, Maxie, how are you today?" Lisa said warmly.

"What's with her?" Max muttered the minute the door closed behind Lisa. "She actually smiled at me."

Shanon blushed. "I was just talking to her about being nicer to you," she explained.

"Gosh"—Max giggled uneasily—"how embarrassing." Tossing her trombone case into the corner, she smoothed out her bed. "Am I such a horrible person that you have to ask your best friend to do you a favor and be nice to me?"

"That's not how it happened," Shanon said hastily. "Lisa's been kind of moody with everybody, including me and her boyfriend."

"She's probably upset about the thing with her parents," Max said thoughtfully. "I can understand that, I guess. Having your parents divorce is a horrible thing. I only wish she didn't hate me so much."

"She doesn't hate you!" Shanon insisted. "How could she, when she hardly knows you?"

Max crossed her eyes and made a face. "You're right," she said. "Lisa has yet to learn what a goofball I am."

"You're not a goofball," Shanon said with a chuckle.

Suddenly Max turned serious. "Do you want me to switch rooms with Lisa?" she asked abruptly.

"You'd really do that?" Shanon asked, taken aback.

"If you'd be happier," Max said, shrugging. "After all, you and Lisa were friends first."

Shanon thought for a moment. She really did want to live with Lisa again, but Max had become a close friend as well.

"Do you really want to move out of the suite and live by yourself?" Shanon asked hesitantly.

"Not really," Max admitted. "At home I'm used to living with a lot of people. And I'd really miss you and Amy," she blurted out. "But if you don't want me for a roommate anymore, since Lisa is back. . . ." Her voice trailed off.

Shanon looked into Max's green eyes, and Max lowered her lashes. "Thanks for making the offer," Shanon said, "but I don't want you to leave the suite unless you really want to."

"Great," Max said with a smile.

"It's tough that Lisa can't live with us this year," said Shanon, "but someday I'm sure that we'll all live together again—all five of us."

While Shanon and Max were having this conversation, Lisa was stretched out on the gaily colored quilt that covered the bed in the privacy of her own room. In her hand was the letter she had just written to Rob. *He's so sweet,* she thought, imagining her pen pal's dreamy blue eyes. *He's so handsome . . . even with that dumb haircut!* But most of all, Lisa reminded herself, Rob was a good person.

She reached for an envelope just as Palmer poked her head in the door.

"Can I come in?" Palmer asked.

"Sure," said Lisa.

"I just got all the info on Greg Proudfoot in the mail!" Palmer bubbled. "He's definitely the Ardie I want to invite me to the dance marathon!"

"Did Greg write you a letter?" Lisa asked curiously.

"Not exactly," Palmer replied. "I just heard from Holbrook Wellington, that kind of nerdy guy at Ardsley. Holbrook has a crush on me, so he'll do anything I ask him to do. Listen," she said eagerly. . . .

Dear Palmer,

I hope that your friend finds the information that I have obtained on one Gregory Proudfoot, 6'2" macho-type football player, helpful:

Greg lives in Dana Hall. He is not much of a talker or much of a student. His only claim to fame is being quarterback on the football team. Hailing from the state of Texas, "Big" Greg, as some of his pals refer to him, is from an oil family. Greg eats like a horse according to the dietician.

If you need any more research done or change your mind about coming to the dance marathon, write to me again.

At your service,
Holbrook Wellington IV

"Are you sure Greg is the one you want to invite you to the dance?" Lisa said. "It sounds like he's not very smart."

"Who cares about that?" exclaimed Palmer. "He's the quarterback of the football team! That's much more important. Besides," she added slyly, "if he comes from an 'oil family,' his allowance must be humongous."

"You have loads of money from your own family," Lisa pointed out. "How come you care about money so much?"

"It's just something I've been brought up to expect," Palmer explained. "When Sam O'Leary was my pen pal, he never had any money. It got kind of boring after a while."

"You're so funny, Palmer," Lisa said. "I'll never understand you as long as I live."

"What's there to understand?" Palmer giggled. "I've chosen Greg Proudfoot to be my date for the dance."

"I thought he had to choose you," Lisa said.

"Minor detail." Palmer shrugged. "After you write to Rob again and tell him how wonderful I am, Greg is bound to be interested."

"Hold on," Lisa said, sitting up on her bed. "I've just had a major, major problem with Rob. Thanks to this letter I've just written him, things will probably get patched up. But I don't know if Rob is going to want to keep carrying messages between you and Greg. Rob and Greg may not even be friends."

"They're both on the football team," Palmer insisted. "They must spend every day of their lives together. Come on, Lisa—just do me one more favor."

"Okay, I guess," Lisa relented. "What is it?"

"Add a line or two from me to Greg in your letter to Rob," Palmer pleaded. "It couldn't be simpler. You might

46

also put in a good word for me yourself with Rob to make it believable."

"I'm drawing the line there," Lisa stated firmly. "I'm not going to clutter up my letter to Rob with a bunch of baloney about how gorgeous *you* are. I will send a short message to Greg for you, though," she said generously.

"Thank you! Thank you!" Palmer cried, jumping up and down.

"I know how important having a boyfriend is," Lisa said sincerely. "Are you sure that Greg's the one you want, though?" she asked as an afterthought. "Holbrook said he eats like a horse."

"Holbrook just said that because he guessed that I was getting information for myself and not for my friend," Palmer said. "Holbrook is in love with me, so he made up those things about Greg to throw me off the track."

"I suppose you have it all figured out," Lisa said, lifting an eyebrow.

"Count on it," Palmer said with a toss of her blond hair. "When it comes to boys, I know exactly what I'm doing."

Dear Rob,
I was so dumb to get that angry about the date at Lulu's. I didn't understand how much work it is for you to be on the football team. I know that one day soon we will get together—alone—in a beautiful, quiet *place. Then we will be able to talk about our true feelings for each other. Until then, I will be thinking about you. I am very sorry if my last letter hurt your feelings.*

Love always and always,
Your Lisa!

P.S. *Your haircut is not all that bad.*
P.P.S. *Tell Greg Proudfoot that Palmer Durand says it is urgent that he get in touch with her. So Greg should write her a letter.*

Dear Lisa,

I'm glad you're not still mad at me. I really am sorry that our date at Lulu's was such a bust. I didn't even buy you a lousy soda. I have so much football on my mind. We beat Pewter Academy in our first game, 14–7. Hope to see you sometime.

Love,
Rob

P.S. *When I told him that Palmer said "Hi," Greg Proudfoot didn't say* anything. *I'm not sure he remembers who she is.*

CHAPTER SIX

The following Saturday, all five girls were out on their bikes again. The weather was still unseasonably hot. With water bottles and knapsacks slung over their shoulders and dressed in shorts or bike pants and sleeveless T-shirts, Shanon, Lisa, Amy, Palmer, and Max were the picture of summer.

"I'm pooped," Shanon called from behind. "Where are we going, anyway?" she shouted, following the pack and turning right. "This isn't the road to the library!"

"I know!" Lisa called out gleefully from her place next to Palmer in the lead. "It's the road to Ardsley Academy!"

"Ardsley!" Shanon gasped. "Why? How? Whose idea was that?"

"I think Palmer and Lisa thought of it," Max announced, whizzing along on Shanon's right. "I thought we were going to the library, too. That's what we put on our passes. But somewhere along the way there was a change of plan."

"Palmer couldn't stand the fact that Greg Proudfoot didn't remember her," Amy yelled over her shoulder. "She

49

told me about it just when we were leaving. I told her she was crazy to try it! But you know Palmer. I'm dying to know how she thinks we're going to get in at the gate!"

"Do you have to have special permission to go onto the Ardsley campus?" Max asked nervously. The thought of seeing Paul threw her into high gear, but she didn't want to get into trouble for it.

"As far as I know, you do need permission," Amy replied. "What's wrong?" she shouted at Shanon. "You look miserable. Don't you want to see Mars?"

"Sure," Shanon croaked, struggling to keep up. "I just hope we can get permission to go on campus. I'm also getting thirsty—Lisa and Palmer have us biking about a hundred miles an hour."

"Want to stop?" Amy asked.

"That's okay," Shanon puffed. "We're almost there."

Ardsley Academy had a formal entrance, just like Alma Stephens did. The girls pedaled up the driveway and stopped a short distance from the gate.

"Have some water," Lisa said, tossing her canteen to Shanon.

"Thanks," Shanon said weakly. Having dropped her bike down on the grass, she flopped herself beneath the nearest tree.

Lisa, on the other hand, didn't seem the least bit tired. "Isn't this the most sensational idea ever?" she said, her face flushed with excitement and exertion.

"Nice of you to spring it on us, without asking what we thought about it," Shanon muttered.

"If I had asked you, you would probably have said 'No,'" Lisa replied with a laugh. "Whereas I am totally wired at the thought of seeing Rob! I don't have to wait until football season is over after all. I can see him at his practice!"

"If we can get in," warned Amy.

"Leave it to me," said Palmer, breezing by in her turquoise biking outfit. Adjusting her sunglasses, she took a few steps toward the entrance, then peered in at the gate. "It looks like we can just walk in," she said hopefully.

"There's no guard at the gate?" asked Lisa.

Palmer squinted. "I don't see one."

"Great," said Amy. "Let's go."

The five girls walked with their bikes onto the Ardsley campus.

"Gee," Max said, "that was easy."

"Now all we have to do is find the football field," Amy said cheerfully.

"Hold it there!" a voice rang out.

The girls turned abruptly. A gray-haired guard stepped out of a small guardhouse.

"Oh, no," Shanon moaned.

"Rats," Lisa murmured. "There *is* a guard!"

"Can I help you, young ladies?" the man asked, approaching them. All five girls froze.

"We, uh, we have to get a message to the football team," Palmer managed to sputter. "It's urgent."

The guard cocked his head. "Urgent, eh? You girls from Alma Stephens?"

"Yes, we are," Shanon gulped.

"I thought so," the guard said, nodding.

"Can we take a message to the football team?" Palmer asked sweetly.

"Not today," the man replied. "The team's not here."

"Not here?" Lisa wailed.

51

"They're over at St. Paul's," the guard explained. "I hope they beat the socks off them."

Palmer sighed and turned toward the gate again. The other four girls followed.

"Darn!" Lisa grumbled, slamming her bike down the driveway. "I'm beginning to hate football! We went to all this trouble and Rob's not even here!"

"I think the guard might actually have let us in," Shanon observed in amazement. "Don't worry," she comforted Lisa. "You and Rob will get together—just wait!"

A car glided slowly past them on the road. The sun was high in the sky, and inside the Ardsley walls the clock was chiming twelve o'clock.

"Time for lunch," Amy announced. "I'm hungry." She squinted down the road. "What shall we do?"

"It's too far to bike into town," Shanon said.

"We've got plenty of peanut butter and jelly sandwiches with us," said Max. "Let's have a picnic!"

"But where?" said Lisa. "I was really looking forward to being with Rob today," she added. "I packed a sandwich for him, too. I thought maybe after football practice. . . ."

"Let's just ride awhile!" Amy suggested, hopping onto her bike. "Maybe we can find a shady spot we've never seen before."

A delicious gust of cool air swirled around them as the group took off down the country road.

"A breeze!" Shanon cried, having gotten her second wind.

"Race you!" yelled Amy.

"Where to?" Maxie said, putting her foot to the pedal.

"Who knows?" Amy replied. "To anywhere!"

"To the nearest shopping mall!" Palmer joked.

52

"To the nearest oasis!" Shanon piped up.

In sudden high spirits, the pack was off!

"Where *are* we headed?" Max shouted giddily.

"We're headed for adventure!" Lisa cried out, letting go of her disappointment about Rob. She threw Shanon a smile. "Are you up for it?"

Shanon smiled back. "Lead on!"

Cutting loose from roommate problems, parent problems, and boy problems, the five Foxes whizzed off into nowhere, relishing their freedom and the Indian summer.

CHAPTER SEVEN

———⬥———

The girls turned off the main highway. Following Amy down an unfamiliar dirt road, they found themselves at a dead end. There in an immense clearing was a rolling lawn and a large, elegant, red brick house.

"I've never seen a house like that in my life!" Shanon gasped.

"House?" Lisa said. "You mean *mansion!* Whoever lives here must be a millionaire."

"I suppose the road we just followed must be their driveway," reasoned Max.

"It is!" Palmer said excitedly. "This is Ursula Baldwin's house! I know her! She's a friend of mine!"

"You actually know the person who lives here?" Lisa gulped.

"She's a movie star," Palmer said excitedly. "She just moved into Brighton last year, but this year she's making a movie in Europe."

"Wow," said Shanon, staring at the house on the hill. "A movie star in Brighton. I think I read about it somewhere."

"It was in all the fan magazines," Palmer said knowledgeably. "Ursula is a very private person. She's been married three times and is a Pisces."

"You seem to know an awful lot about her," observed Lisa.

Palmer tossed her head coyly. "Like I said, she's a friend of mine."

"Oh, my gosh!" said Shanon, pointing ahead. "Look at Amy! She's practically in the front yard!"

"Hey, Amy!" Max yelled.

With a grin on her face, Amy turned. "Come on up!" she cried. "This place is amazing!"

"It's also private property!" Shanon warned.

"Relax," Palmer said, heading up the hill. "I'm sure nobody's home. Ursula's in Europe."

"Then she wouldn't mind our looking around," Lisa said, tromping eagerly onto the lawn.

"She might," Max cautioned. "In fact, a place like this might have a big Doberman pinscher guarding it."

"Ursula doesn't have a Doberman," Palmer called over her shoulder. "She likes small animals like poodles, and her hobbies are chess and horseback riding."

"Come on, slowpokes!" Lisa urged from up ahead. "Wait until you see the pool they've got here!"

Shanon and Max left their bikes at the edge of the driveway and climbed the hill leading to the manicured front yard. Rounding the side of the house to the back terrace, they found Palmer, Lisa, and Amy already seated on white wicker lounges, facing an enormous heart-shaped pool.

"What an amazing pool!" Max said, rushing forward. "Even though it's heart-shaped, it's got to be Olympic size! I wish I could jump in this minute!"

"Me, too!" Amy agreed.

"Nobody seems to be home," Lisa commented, looking around the grounds.

"There aren't any cars around either," Amy pointed out.

"Why should there be?" said Palmer. "Ursula will be in Sweden for at least two months this fall. The man who is directing her is her fiancé," she volunteered.

"What a life," Shanon sighed, wandering around the terrace. She and Lisa peeked into the back windows. "Gosh, it's like a museum in there," she said, taking in the big, beautifully furnished living room.

"It looks just like something in a magazine," Lisa breathed.

"Ursula has one of the most famous decorators in the United States," Palmer said proudly. "I think she uses the same woman that Mom does. Anyway, I'm sure her taste is impeccable."

Shanon cleared her throat. "Guess we'd better get out of here."

"What's the rush?" asked Lisa.

"Because we're on private property," Shanon reminded her

Palmer glanced around. "Nobody's here. We're not disturbing anyone."

"Besides," Lisa added, nudging Shanon. "Ursula is Palmer's friend."

"That's right," said Amy, eyeing the pool. "Do you think she'd mind if we went swimming here?"

"I, uh, guess not," Palmer said hesitantly.

"Great!" said Max. "That pool looks so fabulous, I'll even swim in my underwear."

Shanon looked worried. "Suppose somebody comes and asks what we're doing here?"

"We'll say we're friends of Palmer's," Lisa said brightly. "Right, Palmer?"

Palmer blushed. "Sure," she replied. "Any friend of mine is a friend of Ursula Baldwin's, I guess."

"Look!" Amy cried. "There's even a pool house!"

"Wow!" Lisa chimed in from the other side of the terrace. "This is really nice of you, Palmer," she exclaimed, tossing down her knapsack. "It isn't every day that we get to hang out at a mansion!"

She ripped open her lunch. "Want something to eat?" she asked Shanon.

"I am kind of hungry," Shanon said in a shaky voice. "But I'm also kind of nervous eating my lunch on somebody else's terrace."

"Relax," Lisa assured her. "Palmer is Ursula's friend and she says it's okay. Right, Palmer?" she asked.

"Right!" Palmer said.

"I'm going for a swim before I eat!" Max announced, stepping out of her shorts.

"Me, too!" Amy said.

Max dove into the water. "This is incredible!" she squealed. "Aren't the rest of you coming in?"

"You bet!" Palmer replied, heading toward the pool house.

"Me, too!" said Amy. "It's not every day we get to go swimming in the lap of luxury!"

Shanon and Lisa finished their lunches and went swimming with the other three girls. Then all five of them sat on the lawn, giggling as the late afternoon sun dried them off.

"I never want to leave here," Max sighed.

"Wouldn't it be neat if the house belonged to us?" said Amy.

"We could swim in our own private pool every day instead of going to class!" said Lisa.

"Think of the great parties we could throw!" Palmer exclaimed.

"Maybe we will live together in a place like this someday," Shanon said dreamily. "Maybe after we get out of college, we could all get a place just like this. Of course, we'd have to be awfully rich."

"I hope we do all live together after we get out of school," Lisa said earnestly. "Maybe not in a house as big as this, but in a terrific apartment somewhere."

"I wish we all lived together now," Amy chimed in. "Next year, we've definitely got to get a suite big enough for all of us."

"That would be the greatest," Lisa said. She threw a kindly look in Max's direction. "Of course, I don't blame Max for what happened, though."

Max smiled. "Thanks," she said.

"I'm hot again," Amy declared suddenly. She jumped up and ran toward the pool. "Last one in is a rotten egg!"

"Not me!" yelled Lisa, dashing after her.

"Not me either," Shanon squeaked.

"Well, I'm not playing," Palmer announced, fluffing her hair up.

"You are, too!" Max cried, grabbing her arm. And before she knew what was happening, Palmer was dripping wet. Max dove in behind while Lisa, Shanon, and Amy let out loud cheers. They stayed in for a while, enjoying the cool, clear water, swimming laps and splashing one another.

Afterward, they lounged on the terrace.

"I'm glad we found this place," Shanon said, relaxing into the peace and quiet. "But I guess we'd better leave soon."

"Some neighbors might wonder who we are," said Amy.

"Neighbors?" Palmer said breezily. "What neighbors?"

"Oh, no!" moaned Shanon suddenly.

"What's wrong?" asked Lisa.

"I told Maggie that I would pick up a book for her at the Brighton library," she explained.

"It's too late to go to the library now," Max said, squinting up at the sun. "It's going to be dark in an hour or so."

"But the library is where Maggie and Dan thought we were going," Shanon said. "That's what we put down on our passes. But instead we went to Ardsley and then to this place."

"And aren't you glad we did?" Palmer said.

"I guess so," Shanon said weakly. "But what am I going to say when Maggie asks where her book is?"

"Say you forgot," Lisa suggested.

"I hate to lie to Maggie," Shanon said.

"Maybe you could tell the truth," Max suggested.

"The truth?" squawked Palmer. "Are you crazy? We'd get tarred and feathered if Miss Pryn found out we'd tried to sneak into Ardsley. Besides," she added, "I don't want it getting around that we stopped at Ursula Baldwin's house."

"How come?" Max asked. "I thought you said it was okay that we were here."

Palmer's cheeks flamed pink. "It, uh, is okay," she stammered. "Only I don't want other people getting the same idea and using our dream house."

Lisa laughed. "*Our* dream house? Since when does Ursula Baldwin's house belong to us?"

Palmer smiled. "As long as Ursula's in Europe and it's hot like this, we can use the pool whenever we like."

"I don't think we should," said Shanon. "Once is enough."

As soon as they were dressed for the ride back home, the girls began to gather up their things.

"Even if we weren't exactly invited here," Max sighed, looking at the pool, "it sure has been fun."

"It has been," Shanon admitted, "but I still don't know what to tell Maggie."

"Tell her that you wanted to pick up the book, but it slipped your mind," Lisa said helpfully. She gave Shanon a pat on the back. "That really won't be lying. Picking up Maggie's book did slip your mind. You were too busy swimming."

"Okay," Shanon agreed, trying not to feel guilty. "Maggie and Dan would be pretty upset if I told them the truth, that we dropped by somebody else's house when they weren't even at home."

"The way you talk about Maggie and Dan, you'd think they were old fuddy-duddies," said Amy. "I'm sure if they were our age and had found a neat swimming pool that belonged to a friend who happened to be out of town, they would have taken a swim, too."

"You're probably right," Max agreed. "Dan and Maggie are the coolest grown-ups I know. I can't wait to see what their baby turns out to be like!"

"Well *I* can!" Palmer said, starting down the hill.

"Don't you like babies?" Lisa asked.

"All they do is cry," Palmer replied.

"Still, though," said Shanon, "it must be pretty exciting."

Max smiled. "Remember, we've got first dibs on baby-sitting."

"You can have it," Palmer snorted. "I wouldn't be caught dead taking care of a baby."

At the edge of the driveway, the girls picked up their bicycles. For a long moment, they stood staring up the hill toward the big house.

"What a neat place," said Shanon.

"Too bad we have to go back to school," said Lisa. "I even forgot about not seeing Rob when I was at Ursula Baldwin's house."

"I even forgot the hour exams we have coming up," Amy chimed in.

"Hour exams!" Palmer groaned. "Don't remind me."

"Let's go," Max said. "I've got some chemistry problems to do before dinner."

With a parting glance at the house on the hill, the girls biked rapidly down the road with Amy in the lead. It had been an unforgettable day.

CHAPTER EIGHT

"Ready to go to study hall?" Max asked, skipping down the library steps.

"If my arms don't break first," Shanon said, balancing her heavy stack of books. "I wonder where Lisa is. She was supposed to be at the library this morning, too."

"Maybe she's with Amy in study hall," Max suggested. She squinted across the yard. "Here comes Palmer."

"Guess what, everybody!" Palmer yelled, running onto the sidewalk. "I got mail!"

"Congratulations," laughed Max.

"It's something I've really been waiting for!" Palmer said.

"Did you get an invitation to the Ardsley dance?" Shanon asked, assuming that nothing else could make Palmer so happy.

"Not precisely an invitation," Palmer said, sitting down on the steps, "but from the sound of this letter I'd say that I'll definitely be getting one in the very near future."

"Who's the letter from?" Max asked curiously.

"Only from the quarterback of the Ardsley football team," Palmer said smugly.

"You got a letter from Greg Proudfoot?" Lisa cried, walking up to the group. "This must be our lucky day," she said, beaming. "I just got a letter, too—from Rob!"

"Wow," said Shanon. "Rob wrote to you again?!"

"This time he wants a date," Lisa said brightly.

"A date!" Palmer exclaimed. "How lucky! If you let me read your letter from Rob, I'll let you read my letter from Greg."

The girls giggled and exchanged envelopes.

"Let's head for the study hall," Shanon said. "Amy's waiting for us."

"This is a good letter!" Palmer said as the group walked across campus.

"Read it out loud," Lisa prodded.

Dear Lisa,

Next Thursday, I will have an afternoon off. Maybe we can meet at Lulu's again. What do you think?

Love,
Rob

P.S. St. Paul's beat us 15 to 3, but we're still hanging in there.

"Where do you think we should meet next Thursday?" Lisa asked the other girls. "At Lulu's again or at Figaro's?"

"I don't think you can meet him anywhere next Thursday," Shanon replied, "unless you want to miss Maggie and Dan's Book Talk."

Lisa's face fell. "Is the Book Talk next Thursday?"

"We're discussing *Watership Down*," Max reminded her.

"Well, I certainly wouldn't miss a real date with my boyfriend just for some boring Book Talk," Palmer huffed, eyeing Lisa significantly.

"Why don't you combine them?" Max offered helpfully.

Lisa looked puzzled. "I don't get it."

"Maggie told me yesterday that we could invite a guest next Thursday," Max explained.

"Great," said Shanon. "That means I can ask Mars to come."

"I'm definitely inviting Paul," Max said.

Palmer cleared her throat. "Isn't anyone interested in hearing my letter from Greg?"

"Oh, sure," said Lisa.

Dear Palmer,
Rob Williams told me that you said "Hi." So, I decided to say "Hi" back to you. I hope to see you someday.

Take care,
Greg Proudfoot

"Isn't that sensational?" Palmer crowed. "Next thing you know he'll be asking me to the dance."

"Excuse me, but it sounds a little vague to me," Shanon pointed out, trying to be diplomatic.

"It all depends on how you read it," Palmer countered. "Maybe Greg's shy. Maybe when he says 'Hi,' what he really means to say is that he likes me. And he did say he hoped to see me again someday," she insisted. "Maybe he means on the night of the dance."

"Or maybe next Thursday," Max said helpfully. "Maybe you and Greg can come to Maggie and Dan's together to discuss *Watership Down*."

"Hmmm," Palmer said. "I think for our first date we should do something more exciting. Besides, I haven't actually read that book yet." She turned to Lisa. "Are you going to invite Rob to Maggie and Dan's?"

"I have to think about it," said Lisa as they entered the study hall. "Rob wants to meet me someplace like Lulu's or Figaro's, not at a Book Talk."

The room was very crowded, but Amy had saved them some seats. As Shanon and Max sat down and opened their notebooks, Amy looked up from the math she'd been studying.

"Hi," she whispered.

"Hi," Palmer said, settling into her seat. "I got a letter from—"

"I'll read it later," Amy said quietly. "I'm right in the middle of this problem."

Palmer turned to Lisa, who had opened her Latin book and was staring off into space. Then she pulled out a list of spelling words and let out a sigh.

A younger girl tiptoed over to the table. "Are you using that encyclopedia?" she said softly, pointing to a volume in front of Amy.

Amy shook her head no and Shanon and Max both looked up as the girl whispered "Thanks!" and walked away with the book.

"Who's that?" asked Max.

"Her name is Maida," Amy replied. "She lives in Cabot Hall and she's really intelligent."

Lisa slammed her Latin book shut. "I'm taking a study break," she announced.

"A break?" said Shanon. "You just started."

"I just can't study right now," said Lisa. "The weather's too nice. See you later."

"Wait up," Palmer said. "I need a break, too."

Snatching up their belongings, Lisa and Palmer tiptoed out of the study hall.

"What a dorky scene!" Palmer cried once they were outside.

"Ugh," Lisa agreed. "Study hall really is boring."

Palmer rolled her eyes. "You'd think the way everybody was whispering that somebody had died."

Lisa giggled. "People really do get serious around here at exam time." She looked up at the sky and smiled. "Let's go to my room," she said mischievously. "I've got a stash of chocolate candy bars there."

"I shouldn't," Palmer said. "Chocolate makes my skin break out."

"Mine, too," Lisa said, "but sometimes it's worth it!"

Inside Lisa's single, the girls sat cross-legged on the bed.

"So where do you think I should go on my date with Rob?" Lisa asked Palmer.

"Not to the Book Talk," Palmer said, turning her thumb down.

"I agree," Lisa said, munching on a candy bar. "But how can I get out of going?"

"Just say you have something important to do at the Brighton library," Palmer suggested, glancing at the posters on Lisa's wall. "Or, better still, tell Maggie that you're going to the Brighton museum for that art show! She'd have to let you go. After all," Palmer reasoned, "art is just as important as books."

Lisa settled back against her pillow. "Okay," she said. "I'll write to Rob and tell him to meet me at Figaro's."

"Don't go there," Palmer warned. "Figaro's has changed."

"How?" Lisa asked.

"At the end of last year when we went there, it was totally mobbed with kids from Brighton High," Palmer explained. "You couldn't even get a booth."

Lisa wrinkled her nose. "That means Rob and I won't have any privacy. It'll be just as bad as it was at Lulu's." She sighed. "I want to do something really special with Rob on this date. I want it to be in some quiet, romantic place where we can talk to each other and have fun, not in some dumb pizza parlor where everybody else is hanging out."

"But where are you going to find a place like that in Brighton?" Palmer asked.

"I know!" Lisa said impulsively. "I could take Rob to Ursula Baldwin's house. If it's a warm day like today, we could even go swimming."

"Well, I don't know," Palmer said hesitantly. "Ursula's not there."

"That's the whole point," Lisa squealed. "Just think of it!" She lowered her eyes. "But I guess it wouldn't be right if Rob and I showed up without you there."

"You want me to go on a *date* with you?" Palmer said incredulously.

"Of course not," said Lisa. "I was only saying that if Rob and I did want to go swimming at the Baldwin estate, we couldn't do it alone. You'd have to be there, since you know Ursula Baldwin and we don't."

"Well, I'm not going on a date with you and Rob," Palmer said, rolling her eyes.

"I don't expect you to," said Lisa. "Unless . . ." she continued thoughtfully, "you didn't have to be by yourself and somebody else was there."

"Like who?" asked Palmer.

Lisa leaned over and smiled. "Who do you think?" she said. "Greg Proudfoot!"

Palmer gasped. "You mean a double date?"

"Why not?" said Lisa. "Since you know Ursula so well, I'm sure she wouldn't mind if the two of us had a date at her pool."

Palmer gulped. "I guess not."

"Please," Lisa begged. "Don't you see? It'll be perfect! I can write to Rob and get him to bring Greg. Greg did say in his letter that he wanted to see you again."

"Yeah, he did," Palmer agreed, blue eyes shining. "And it would only be for a couple of hours, right?"

"We probably couldn't get a town pass for any longer than that," said Lisa. She looked at Palmer eagerly. "So, will you do it? Will you let me invite Rob and Greg to Ursula Baldwin's?"

"Are you sure Greg will come?" Palmer asked.

"I'll tell Rob that it has to be that way," Lisa promised.

Palmer grinned. "Ursula's pool really is great."

"We can pack a picnic lunch," Lisa exclaimed.

"And bring some music and our bathing suits," bubbled Palmer. She got up and smiled at herself in the mirror. "We can have a real pool party!"

"A real date!" said Lisa.

"A double date!" shrieked Palmer. "Only, we'd better ask the guys not to tell anybody about it," she said.

"How come?" Lisa asked.

Palmer shrugged. "Because it's our business."

"Okay," Lisa said, rummaging in her desk for a pen and some stationery. "Wait until Shanon and Amy find out," she said. "They'll be sorry they asked Nikos and Mars to that boring Book Talk."

Palmer blinked. "I don't think we should tell them either."

"Not tell Shanon?" Lisa said.

"You know how uptight she was the first time we went to Ursula's," said Palmer. "And Max will probably think we should have invited Rob and Greg to the book thing. You know how much she loves Maggie and Dan."

"Okay, if that's the way you want it," Lisa said agreeably.

"It's the way I want it," said Palmer.

Lisa's eyes gleamed with a sense of adventure. "So instead of just being a double date, it'll be a secret double date! Wow!" And picking up her pen, she began to write . . .

CHAPTER NINE

Dear Rob,

This is a chance for us to really be together. Ursula Baldwin is a friend of Palmer's, and she said we can use her pool if we want to. It's really going to be fun! Also, will you please ask Greg to come? Palmer and I would like this to be a double date, since if it wasn't for Palmer we wouldn't be able to use the swimming pool. Unless Greg is able to drop by also, you and I will probably have to have our date somewhere else. Write soon to let me know!

XXXOOO!
Lisa

Dear Mars,

Please come to a Book Talk at Maggie and Dan's in Fox Hall, where we will discuss Watership Down. (If you haven't read the book, come anyway.) Hope your leg is better. Also hope to see you a week from Thursday when the Book Talk will be held.

Love,
Shanon

Dear Nikos,

Heard about the disaster at St. Paul's. You guys still seem to be in good shape, however. Next at-home game I'm definitely getting permission to be there. Actually, we almost saw you last Saturday. We dropped by Ardsley, but the team wasn't there. Maggie and Dan are having a get-together in their apartment next Thursday to discuss Watership Down. We can invite a boy guest, so I hope you can come.

Catch you later,
Amy

Dear Paul,

Please come to a "Book Talk" tea at the home of our faculty residents, Maggie and Dan, next Thursday. I think it will be fun. Watership Down *is an interesting book and Maggie makes great brownies!*

Yours truly,
Max

P.S. I offered to switch rooms with Lisa McGreevy (I only actually told this to Shanon, not to Lisa), but Shanon seems to want me to stay in Suite 3-D.

Hi Shanon,

I'll be there next Thursday to talk about books and sit next to my favorite girl. See you soon.

Love,
Mars

Dear Amy,

I haven't read the book. Hope that's okay. Good timing, the team's off Thursday afternoon. Did you write any more verses to that Back to School song? I liked it, by the way.

Be great to see you again,
Nikos

Max,

Watership Down *is a one of my favorite books! I'll be there!*

Sincerely,
Paul

Dear Lisa,

How come the pool party is top secret? Anyway, wild

horses couldn't keep me away. With this hot weather, an outdoor pool is just what I need. I also need to see you.

Forever,
Rob

P.S. Proudfoot said okay—he'll come.

CHAPTER TEN

———⟶———

Lisa tugged nervously at her turtleneck. Early that Wednesday morning, she'd found a note tacked to her door. Maggie Grayson-Griffith wanted to see her immediately. Now, perched on the worn velvet armchair in Maggie and Dan's apartment, Lisa waited impatiently while the attractive young teacher brewed peppermint tea. In Lisa's first year at Alma, Maggie had been one of her favorite people. Since coming back to school this year, however, she hadn't spent much time with her outside of French class.

"Would you like some sugar in your tea?" Maggie asked graciously.

Lisa nodded yes and watched Maggie gingerly drop two white lumps into a china cup and then pour in some tea.

"Are you trying to dodge us?" Maggie asked, settling down across from her. In the bold flowered shift she was wearing, she looked more pregnant than ever.

Lisa blinked. "I don't know what you mean."

"You didn't come to our Welcome Back tea," Maggie explained, smiling softly.

"Is that why you're giving me tea now?" Lisa joked.

"Not exactly," replied Maggie.

Lisa squirmed in her chair. She couldn't remember when it started, but nowadays she hated being with teachers. In fact, she didn't like being with any grown-ups. One reason she'd been glad to return to boarding school was to get away from her parents.

"How are your mom and dad?" Maggie asked, as if reading Lisa's mind.

Lisa shrugged. "I haven't heard from them in a while. Is that why you asked me down here? Something to do with my parents?"

"Not really," said Maggie. "I can only guess what a difficult year you've just had, with your folks breaking up."

"Did they call and ask you to keep tabs on me?" guessed Lisa.

Maggie shook her head silently.

"Good," said Lisa, "because I'm okay."

"Are you sure?" asked Maggie.

Lisa crossed her legs and jiggled her foot. Maggie was really making her uncomfortable. "Why did you want to see me?" she asked bluntly.

"Dan and I are concerned," Maggie replied, leaning forward. "You've been very preoccupied lately."

"No, I haven't," Lisa said. "I'm really glad to be back at Alma . . . in the state of New Hampshire," she added, thinking of Rob.

"Nevertheless," Maggie pointed out, "you *have* been preoccupied, at least in your classes—those you've attended, at any rate."

Lisa blushed. She knew she hadn't really buckled down

yet. But since no one had said anything, she'd thought they hadn't noticed.

"Mr. Seganish showed me your first hour exam," Maggie went on.

"I messed it up," Lisa said sheepishly. "Next time I'll do better."

"I hope so," said Maggie, "because your math quiz was also a disaster."

"I just don't feel like studying," Lisa admitted. "All I did last year at home was worry. I don't want to think about anything serious."

"No one's asking you to spend all your time studying, but this is a school. Classes are a major part of your life here. You used to be a pretty good student," Maggie reminded her.

"Well, I'm not interested in academics anymore," Lisa said stubbornly.

Maggie sighed. "There are a couple of other things—your comportment, for example."

Lisa's face flamed. "My what?"

"You know we have a dress code here," Maggie explained, "but you seem to be ignoring it lately. And you've been wearing too much makeup in class."

"That makeup rule is stupid," Lisa argued. "And so is the one about wearing skirts."

"That may be," Maggie said sternly. "But they are still the rules. I just don't want to see you get into trouble," she said, softening.

"Everybody's afraid I'm going to get into trouble," Lisa complained. "Don't worry. I can take care of myself."

"I'm sure you can, but we're here to help when you need us," Maggie said, offering Lisa the cookie plate.

Lisa grabbed a cookie and bit into it. "Thanks a lot, but I'm okay," she repeated.

"It would be only normal if you were still upset or angry about your parents' divorce," Maggie said encouragingly.

"I'm not upset!" Lisa snapped, then immediately felt sorry. Maggie was so nice! Lisa knew her teacher was only trying to be helpful. The problem was, Lisa really didn't feel like talking about how awful life was as a kid in a divorced family. Besides, since she'd finally figured out a way to see Rob, she felt great!

"Did you buy all the stuff you need for the new baby?" Lisa asked to change the subject.

"We have something for him or her to sleep in at least," Maggie replied, motioning to a white bassinette in the corner of the room. "There's still a lot to do," she confided, "and Dan has a conference in Philadelphia coming up." There was a brief silence and then Maggie asked, "Have you read *Watership Down,* yet?"

"A little bit," Lisa said. "It's interesting."

Maggie smiled. "I hope you're coming to the Book Talk tomorrow."

"I'm glad you brought that up," Lisa bubbled. "Actually, I was planning to go into Brighton."

"Into Brighton?" Maggie said. "What for?"

"I—I wanted to go to the art show," Lisa said hastily. "It'll only take about an hour."

"That show will be at the museum for the rest of the month," said Maggie.

"But I want to see it now," insisted Lisa.

"Sorry, no pass this time," said Maggie.

"But—I—I have to go!" Lisa said desperately. "I need some important things at the drugstore."

"What things?" asked Maggie.

Lisa's face flamed. "Shampoo and stuff," she said. "I'll be back in time for the Book Talk, I promise. At least I'll try to be back," she hedged.

Maggie shook her head and smiled. "That drugstore owner must be a pretty rich lady," she said. "You and your suitemates must have bought every bottle of shampoo in the store since school started." She got up and walked to the bathroom. "I happen to have an unopened bottle of shampoo," she said, offering it to Lisa.

"It's not the kind I use," Lisa said feebly. She gave Maggie a pleading look. "Please let me go into town. This is serious."

"How can going to the art show and the drugstore be so serious?" asked Maggie.

"Because . . . because it just is," mumbled Lisa.

"I want you to stick around campus for a week or so," Maggie said. Putting an arm around Lisa's shoulders, she walked her to the door. "Concentrate on your studies for a change."

"I will," Lisa promised, "after tomorrow I'll—"

"No," Maggie broke in firmly. "Starting today. Dan and I are here for you, if you ever need to talk anything over," she added, standing in the doorway.

"Thanks," Lisa said, "I'll remember that." And blinking back tears, she fled her teacher's apartment and raced down the hall.

What was she going to do now?

CHAPTER ELEVEN

———————◆———————

"I can't believe we're doing this!" Palmer giggled.

"I'm so excited," Lisa cried, looking up at the sky. "What great weather for a pool party. This is going to be perfect!"

It was half an hour before the Book Talk tea but Palmer and Lisa were long gone. Having managed to bike unnoticed through Alma's front gate, they were on their way to meet Greg and Rob.

"I hope we don't get caught," Palmer shouted into the wind.

"How can we?" Lisa called back gleefully. "Everybody in Fox Hall will be at the Book Talk."

"Do you think Amy, Shanon, and Max believed we were going to the language lab?" Palmer asked.

Lisa looked guilty. "I'm sure Shanon did," she replied. "She felt so sorry for me when I told her that my date with Rob had to be canceled."

"I think Amy thought I was turning over a new leaf when I told her I'd be studying," Palmer said with a chuckle.

"I hated lying to them," Lisa said, "but if this is the only way I can get to see Rob. . . ."

Breathing in the sweet autumn air, the girls coasted down a gentle hill. Beneath their jeans and T-shirts they were both wearing bathing suits. And on the rear of her bicycle, Lisa was carrying two baskets loaded with party food. In her knapsack, Palmer had a radio and some towels.

Lisa felt like singing as they turned in at the Baldwin mansion. "No sign of anybody at home," she said, squinting up the driveway. "Should we walk up? These baskets are heavy."

"Sure," Palmer said. "What a sprint," she panted, wiping her forehead with a handkerchief. "I can't believe how fast we got here."

"I'd sprint around the world to have a real date with Rob!" said Lisa.

The two girls headed straight for the terrace. Palmer quickly pulled out the towels and music, while Lisa unpacked the food. Along with sodas there was popcorn and cupcakes.

"Look at all the yummy food we've got," Lisa said, setting it out on the table. "There's enough for an army!"

"Those flowered napkins and paper cups you brought are just right, too," Palmer said with an approving smile.

"Oh, my gosh," Lisa said suddenly. "The swimming pool . . . It's . . . it's got a thing on it!"

Palmer jerked around and stared at the ugly, thick vinyl tarp that was now covering the beautiful blue water.

"Somebody's put a cover on the pool," Lisa said in dismay.

"That means there's no water," croaked Palmer.

"There's water all right," Lisa said, tapping the tarp with her foot, "but we won't be able to swim in it, because it's underneath this thing."

They bent down to examine the pool cover, but it was securely fastened on all sides. "Well, we can always use it for a dance floor," Palmer quipped, trying to make light of the situation.

But Lisa was worried. "If we can't swim," she said, "what are we going to do?"

"We'll figure out something," Palmer said, scrambling up hastily. "Don't look now," she breathed, "but they're here!"

Lisa followed Palmer's gaze. Sure enough, a few yards away were Rob and Greg. Lisa felt her heart begin to pound.

"Have I got enough lipstick on?" she asked Palmer shrilly.

"Calm down," Palmer hissed. "The way you're acting, you'd think you'd never been on a date before."

"I haven't," Lisa squeaked. "I mean . . . not with Rob, not alone . . . not in a long time. I want everything to be perfect."

"You're not alone. You're with me," Palmer reminded her, putting on a bright smile. "Hi, Greg!" she called out gaily. "Come on up! You're just in time for the party."

Greg and Rob tossed down their bikes.

"Hi, Lisa," Rob called out.

"Hi!" Lisa said, trying not to sound nervous. She took a deep breath and walked forward. Having a panic attack is the last thing she'd expected. After all, she'd known Rob for two years. This date was something she'd planned. But now that it was happening, she felt giddy. What if something went wrong? After all, they weren't even supposed to be there. And now that she was finally going to be alone with Rob, what would she say? All the speeches she'd rehearsed alone in her room that morning had totally deserted her.

She had planned to throw herself in her pen pal's arms and say something like "Rob, it seems as if it's been forever!" but instead she found herself giggling and totally speechless.

"Hi," she said again, managing to get her voice back.

"Hi, yourself," Rob said, blushing slightly. "Nice place you've got here," he added, looking around at the terrace.

"It's Palmer's," Lisa squeaked. "I mean, the house belongs to Palmer's friend," she explained, trying to compose herself. She gave Rob a little smile. His eyes were such a deep blue, she could get lost in them. "Want to . . . to go swimming?" she stammered without thinking.

Rob turned his gaze toward the pool. "I brought my suit," he said, "but it might be a little difficult with that cover on the pool."

"Of course," Lisa agreed, blushing furiously. "Palmer and I were just noticing that. I guess we can't go swimming after all."

Greg Proudfoot grunted.

"I know!" said Rob. "Greg and I can pull off the pool cover, or at least part of it. Come on, Buddy, let's give it a try!"

Lisa and Palmer looked at each other, but before they could say anything the boys had started tugging at the canvas. Within seconds, a corner of the pool was exposed.

"That should do it!" said Rob. "Everybody in the pool!"

"You can change in the pool house," Palmer gulped,

pointing to the green building at the edge of the terrace.

Rob touched Lisa's hand lightly. "See you in a minute," he said, crossing the terrace with Greg.

Lisa threw herself into a deck chair and blew out a breath. "I think I'm going to faint," she said.

"Don't," Palmer warned. "It'll spoil the party."

"Sorry," Lisa apologized, giggling nervously. "Now that my dream has finally come true, I can't seem to believe it."

"Believe it," said Palmer. "We're on a double date, complete with food, boys, and a heart-shaped pool."

When Greg and Rob reappeared, Lisa and Palmer went in to change. By the time they came out in their suits, Rob was already splashing around in the pool. Greg was in front of the table, wolfing down huge handfuls of popcorn. Palmer watched in amazement. He had to be the fastest eater she'd ever seen.

"Come on in!" Rob shouted playfully. "The water's fine."

Feeling a bit calmer, Lisa slipped in beside him. With a flick of her wrist, Lisa splashed some water at Palmer.

"Hey, watch it!" Greg mumbled between mouthfuls. "I'm getting wet."

Palmer smiled. Greg had finally said something!

"What kind of music would you like to hear?" she chirped.

Greg grunted. "Anything," he mumbled.

"Soft rock?" Palmer asked hopefully.

The boy shook his head. "Uh-uh."

"Disco?" Palmer encouraged, snapping her fingers.

Greg shook his head again.

"What about rap?" she asked helplessly.

"That popcorn made me thirsty," he volunteered, ignoring her question. "I think I'll have some soda—and maybe a cupcake."

Palmer turned the radio up a little bit louder and began tapping her foot in time to the music. Greg seemed to be more interested in the food than in her. "I'm a great dancer," she said, tapping faster. She began to bob her head. "I'm definitely into dancing as a physical activity. It's kind of like football. I could dance all night," she exclaimed. "I could even dance in a dance marathon."

Greg burped and covered his mouth a moment too late. "Got anything else to eat?" he asked.

Palmer's eyes widened. The popcorn bowl was almost empty and three cupcakes were gone. "I hear that the food is really good at the Ardsley dances," she said weakly. "Do you go to the dances at Ardsley?"

"Not much," muttered Greg, glancing around. For a moment, his eyes seem to rest on Palmer's hair. "Nice headband," he said awkwardly when he realized she'd caught him staring. "Is it made out of pigskin?"

"No, just regular leather," Palmer said flatly. She glanced over at Lisa helplessly. Getting a dance invitation out of Greg was going to be harder than she'd thought. "Hey, Lisa," she called, "have you and Rob definitely decided to go to the dance marathon?"

"Hmmm, I guess so," Lisa murmured, hardly hearing her. The dance a month away was the last thing on her mind. She was with Rob *now,* and that was what mattered. Side by side in the pool, they smiled at each other and hooked fingers underwater.

"Isn't this great?" said Rob. "If the pool wasn't covered, I'd challenge you to a race."

Lisa smiled. The touch of Rob's hand and the warm

water had finally relaxed her. "A race that I'd win, you big lug," she said mischievously. "Everything is so perfect here. I wish we could stay forever."

"Me, too," Rob said with a grin. "This is one afternoon I'm glad I'm not playing football. . . ."

Back at Fox Hall, the Book Talk was half over. Shanon, Amy, Max, and their pen pals were taking a break.

"I'm so glad that your leg is better," Shanon told Mars. She was also extremely glad to see him for the first time that year. Her short humorous pen pal looked different. He wasn't so short anymore. "You changed over the summer," Shanon added shyly.

"You haven't changed at all," Mars said with a twinkle in his dark eyes. "I like that." He brushed a wisp of hair off Shanon's face. "I can't wait until the next time we get together at the dance marathon."

"Me either," said Shanon.

"Are you still coming to the marathon?" Paul asked Max over near the brownie table.

"I've been practicing my dancing," Max giggled.

"Of course we wouldn't have to dance the whole time," Paul said with a serious look on his face. "I mean . . . we could talk, if you know what I mean. . . ."

"I know what you mean," Max said, flushing with pleasure. She really liked Paul. Having him at the Book Talk made it ten times more exciting for Max than it would have been without him. Reaching for a brownie, she grazed his little finger. An electric charge seemed to flow into her hand. "I'm glad you could come today," she confessed with a blush.

"Me, too," said Paul, turning just as red.

In a corner of the Grayson-Griffiths' crammed apartment, Nikos and Amy were sipping some punch. "I thought you hadn't read *Watership Down,*" Amy said teasingly.

Nikos slipped an arm over her shoulder. "I crammed it. I didn't want to look like an idiot. Of course," he added with a snort, "it would have been nice to go to the real party."

Amy stared. "What real party?" she asked.

Nikos hit his forehead. "Uh-oh," he groaned. "I wasn't supposed to say anything. Just forget I ever mentioned it."

"No deal," Amy said, placing her hands on her hips. "You can't drop a bomb like that and not explain it."

At that moment Paul and Max walked over, along with Shanon and Mars.

"I blew it," Nikos greeted the other boys. "Williams is going to cream me when he finds out I spilled his little secret."

"You told about the pool party?" Mars blurted out. "You're right—Rob is going to cream you."

"What pool party?" Shanon asked innocently.

"I smell a rat," Amy said.

Nikos chortled. "She's your roommate."

"You mean Palmer?" piped up Max in confusion. "What about her?"

Nikos, Mars, and Paul exchanged glances.

"I'm surprised Lisa didn't fill you in," Mars said to Shanon.

"Fill us in on what?" Shanon said impatiently. "What's the big secret?"

"Palmer and Lisa invited Rob and my star quarterback to a private party today," Nikos announced with a grin.

"Actually, when I heard the news I was kind of jealous."

"Swimming in an outdoor pool did sound like fun," Paul said to Max. "Of course, the Book Talk is interesting, too," he added hastily.

"Let me get this straight," Amy said, seething. "Palmer and Lisa took Greg and Rob to Ursula Baldwin's?"

"I don't know whose house it was," Mars said, "but there was a map on the invitation. It's in the middle of the woods somewhere between Ardsley and Alma."

"But that can't be true," Shanon said in a shocked voice. "Right now Lisa and Palmer are studying at the language lab. And Rob isn't here because he has football practice today."

"Sorry to tell you the truth," Mars said gently, "but right now Rob Williams and Lisa are at a pool party."

"This could be serious," said Amy. "It's bad enough they're throwing a secret pool party, but I know for a fact that they didn't have passes. If Maggie or Dan find out they're off campus without permission, they—" Amy gulped and broke off in midsentence as Maggie suddenly appeared at her side.

"We're settling down for the second half," Maggie said softly.

The girls looked at each other. From the serene look on her face, it was obvious that the teacher hadn't overheard their conversation.

"How do you like the discussion so far?" Maggie asked the boys in the group.

"Wonderful," Paul said earnestly.

Maggie turned to Shanon. "Where's Lisa?"

Shanon's eyes bugged out. "She's, uh . . . she's, uh. . . ."

"She's at the language lab," Max piped up.

"With Palmer," Amy added.

"Sorry they had to miss this," Maggie said, "but at least they're studying."

Max nodded. "They felt that they had to. They—"

Max's explanation was cut short by Dan Griffith, calling from the other side of the room. "Let's get started on part two!" he said good-naturedly.

"Hurry," Maggie said. "Let's take our seats."

Shanon found it impossible to concentrate on the rest of the discussion. Her mind was spinning. She felt so many things: concern, confusion, betrayal. Why hadn't Lisa confided in her friends?

"What's wrong?" Mars whispered.

Shanon squeezed his hand. "I'm worried," she said. "Lisa's going to get into trouble, and so is Palmer."

"Relax," Mars breathed in her ear. "Rob told me the party was only supposed to last an hour. Lisa will probably be back before the talk's over."

Shanon swallowed. "I hope you're right."

While Shanon was worrying back at Alma Stephens, Palmer and Lisa were in the pool house, happily changing back into their biking clothes.

"Isn't this terrific?" said Lisa. "Everything is working out so perfectly. Rob and I have hardly said a word to each other," she confided, "but we're having so much fun."

"Greg and I haven't said much to each other either," said Palmer; "at least, Greg hasn't said much to me."

"Holbrook told you he wasn't much of a talker," Lisa reminded her.

"Hmmm," said Palmer. "Holbrook also said he eats like

a horse. He was right about that, too. Greg finished every bit of the popcorn."

Lisa giggled.

"But he's still the cutest boy I've ever seen," Palmer said blithely. "Did you notice his muscles?"

"How could I not?" Lisa teased. "But muscles aren't everything."

"I'm sure Greg is a great person, too," Palmer said. "All I have to do is get to know him," she added as the two girls stepped out of the pool house.

"Where are the boys?" Palmer asked, glancing around the empty terrace.

"They haven't left," Lisa said, "because their bikes are still here. Rob," she called nervously, "where are you?"

Rob's voice came out of nowhere. "We're in here!" he shouted.

"In where?" Lisa yelled in confusion.

"Here," Rob said, suddenly appearing in the doorway of the mansion. "Greg had to use the bathroom," he explained. "This house is awesome!"

"Gr-Greg is in the house?" Palmer stammered. "But there's a bathroom in the pool house."

"You girls were in there so long," Rob teased, "poor Greg couldn't wait. The door was unlocked, so. . . ."

"It was unlocked?" Palmer said, rushing up the path. "Did an alarm go off?"

"Why should an alarm go off?" Lisa asked, wide-eyed.

"No, reason," Palmer said, darting away. "I'd better go inside and see what's keeping Greg."

Rob reached for Lisa's hand. "Come on!" he said. "There's something I want to show you!"

CHAPTER TWELVE

"Some pad," Greg announced, coming out of the powder room. "I think it's neat that you know the owner," he told Palmer.

"You do?" Palmer said hopefully.

"Can I see the rest of the place?" Greg asked.

"Sure," Palmer replied. "Why not? Nobody's here and it'll only take a couple of minutes."

"Is it okay that we're inside?" asked Lisa.

"Sure it is," Greg replied, flashing Palmer a goofy grin. "Palmer's friend lives here. How about starting with the kitchen?" he suggested.

Palmer shrugged and giggled and she and Greg wandered off to the kitchen, while Lisa and Rob headed in the other direction toward the living room.

"Wow, is this ever gorgeous!" Lisa exclaimed as she and Rob walked into the enormous front room. "Look at all the paintings on the walls," she said. "And look how pretty the rugs are," she whistled, glancing down at the spotless ivory carpeting.

"Look at this chess set," Rob said, pulling her over to a

table in the far corner with a huge marble chess set on it. "It's what I wanted to show you," he explained. "I've never seen such a big set before. Want to play?" he asked, smiling at her.

Lisa giggled. "At a time like this, you want to play chess?"

Rob took her in his arms. "I guess I can think of more exciting things to do," he said.

"Listen, you mustn't ever tell anybody that we've been here," Lisa said.

"How come?" Rob asked.

Lisa blushed. "Palmer and I kind of sneaked away without permission," she confessed.

"Gosh," said Rob, "I hope you don't get into trouble."

"We won't," Lisa assured him. "Everyone at Fox Hall is at a Book Talk. They'll never miss us. Besides, they all think we're studying."

"I promised I wouldn't tell anybody about our top secret date," he said, glancing away guiltily. "And I won't. At least not anyone who would get you into trouble," he mumbled under his breath.

"What did you say?" asked Lisa.

Rob glanced away. "Oh, nothing. . . ."

"Anyone want a snack?" Palmer asked, coming into the living room with a big bowl of potato chips.

"Where did you find those?" Lisa asked.

"In the kitchen," explained Palmer. "Greg was hungry. There are all kinds of goodies in there. I'm sure Ursula will never miss these."

She put the bowl down on the coffee table. "We'd better not get any of these on the floor," she said, looking a little nervous.

Lisa crossed over to her. "How are things going with Greg?" she whispered. "He seems to be talking more."

"He is," Palmer said flatly. "But he hasn't said anything particularly interesting. And as soon as we got into the kitchen, he shut up again. He's in there now, checking out the refrigerator," she said, rolling her eyes.

Lisa giggled. "Maybe they don't feed him at Ardsley."

"Listen, Lisa," Palmer said, grabbing her friend's arm. "I think we'd better get out of here in a few minutes."

"Can't we stay a little longer?" Lisa begged. She glanced at Rob, who was on the other side of the room looking at some pictures on the wall. "Rob and I have hardly had a chance to talk," she said.

Palmer's eyelids fluttered nervously. "I don't know," she said. "I think we should—"

Just then Greg walked into the room, carrying a liter of grape soda. "Where are the glasses?" he asked Palmer.

"Outside," Palmer said hastily. "There are a bunch of paper cups on the terrace, remember?"

"There are some plastic ones back here," Lisa offered, crossing behind the bar.

"Great," Greg said, giving the soda bottle a sudden twist. "Bring them out."

"Watch out!" Palmer said. "You're going to—"

They all watched in horror as the grape soda spewed into the air and tiny drops of purple rained down on the arm of Ursula Baldwin's pale peach couch and ivory carpet.

"Oh, no," moaned Lisa.

"This is gross!" Palmer exclaimed, running out of the room. "I'll go get a sponge."

Greg hung his head. "I'll go with you," he grunted, trailing behind her.

"Palmer seems kind of nervous," Lisa observed.

"I've been feeling a little nervous myself," Rob admitted. He looked deep into her eyes and then kissed her. "I couldn't have our date end without doing that."

Lisa smiled. "I'm so glad you could come today," she said. "I really felt so weird being back in New Hampshire and not being able to see you."

"You had a rough year," he said gently.

Lisa sighed. "I've been trying not to think about it."

"Sounds like a good idea," Rob said sympathetically.

"I've been goofing off in my subjects, too," Lisa admitted.

"You've still got time to make it up," Rob said. "The school year's only beginning. Wow!" he exclaimed, looking over her shoulder. "Get a load of that television!"

Lisa turned to see what he was talking about. On the far side of the room was a giant screen.

"Mind if I turn it on for a minute?" Rob asked, already heading that way. "This afternoon, Lawrence Taylor's on *Scrimmage Talk.*"

"*Scrimmage Talk?*" Lisa echoed.

"It's a TV show about football," Rob said, clicking on the set. "I'll only check it out for a minute. L.T. is one of my favorite players. . . ."

Meanwhile, back in the kitchen, Palmer was rummaging through the utility pantry. "I think I see a bottle of stain remover," she called out to Greg.

The big jock ambled over to see. "Where is it?" he asked.

"That little bottle next to the can," Palmer directed.

As Greg reached for the bottle, Rob burst into the room, followed close behind by Lisa. "Hey, Greg," Rob called. "*Scrimmage Talk* is on!"

"Great," said Greg, swinging around. Lisa jumped at the

sound of glass hitting the floor. "Sorry," Greg muttered, looking down at the broken bottle by his feet. "I guess I kind of knocked that over."

"Oh, no!" wailed Palmer. "It looks like soap," she said, examining the liquid on the floor.

"Maybe you can use it to get the soda off the carpet," Rob giggled.

"This is no time for joking," Palmer snapped at him. And pulling Lisa to the side of the room, she said, "Excuse me, I have to talk to Lisa."

"Sure," Rob replied agreeably. "We'll go check out the football program."

"We're in really big trouble," Palmer confessed once the boys had left.

"I'm sure we'll be able to get the soda off the rug," Lisa said sympathetically.

"We'd better," said Palmer. "We can't let anybody know that we've been in here. They may be able to trace us," she squawked, her eyes filled with panic.

"What are you talking about, Palmer?"

Palmer's face turned white. "There's something I have to tell you," she said, looking at a spot two inches above Lisa's head. "I—I don't really know Ursula Baldwin."

"What?" Lisa gasped. "You mean we're in somebody else's house and you don't even know them?"

"I kind of know her," Palmer breathed, breaking out into a cold sweat. "My mom went to school with her and when I read in a magazine that she had bought this house, I thought—"

"You thought what?" Lisa demanded.

"I thought that one day I would come by and introduce myself," Palmer sputtered. "My mom and she were good friends and when I saw the picture of the house in the magazine and how cool it looked and then when we found it that day we were out biking. . . . I didn't think it would do any harm," she trailed off helplessly. "The magazine said that Ursula was in Europe. But now that we've spilled soda on the carpet and—"

"Don't say another word," Lisa gulped. "We're wasting time. We've got to get out of here. It's bad enough that we've sneaked away from the dorm." She glanced at the kitchen clock in alarm. "Oh, my gosh," she choked, "the Book Talk is over! And I just thought of something else."

"What?" asked Palmer.

Lisa swallowed. "There must be a caretaker somewhere around here."

"Caretaker?" asked Palmer.

"*Some*body had to put the tarp on the swimming pool," Lisa said ominously just as the boys walked back into the kitchen.

"You should see L.T.!" Rob said excitedly. "He—"

"We haven't got time," Lisa cut him off. "Here's a broom," she said, racing to the pantry.

"I'll find a mop," said Palmer. "After we sweep up the glass, we can mop the soap."

"Want some help?" Greg asked, ambling over to the utility cabinet.

"No, stay away!" Palmer commanded. "I just don't want you to—to break anything else," she stammered in explanation.

"I was thinking about how much you like dancing," Greg mumbled, shifting his feet awkwardly.

Palmer gazed at him in shock. "What?"

"Maybe you want to go to the Ardsley dance marathon," he suggested.

Grabbing the mop, Palmer glared. Greg Proudfoot may

have been cute, but he was boring. And thanks to him Ursula Baldwin's carpet and couch were stained with grape soda and the kitchen floor had glass and soap all over it. Not only that, but he didn't eat like a horse—he ate like a pig!

"No thank you," she said coolly. "I don't think I'm interested in going to the dance marathon."

"There's quite a storm brewing outside," Rob announced from the kitchen window. "The yard is really a mess."

"What do you mean?" Lisa asked, dashing over to look out the window. The sky had gotten darker and the wind had picked up. The whole terrace was strewn with flowered napkins and cups.

"Yikes," she squeaked, "more cleanup." She turned to Rob. "I hate to say this, but the date is over."

"So soon?" said Rob.

"You have to go, too," Palmer told Greg.

"But *Scrimmage Talk* is still on," Greg protested.

"Too bad," Palmer said. "The date is over."

As Palmer shooed the boys out the side door, Rob grabbed Lisa's hand and pulled her onto the lawn.

"I wish I didn't have to leave yet," he said.

"We've been here a long time," Lisa said nervously, "and I don't want you to get into trouble."

"I won't get into trouble," said Rob. "I've got permission to be off campus."

Lisa sighed. "But *I* don't. Palmer and I have to get out of here soon, so. . . ."

They locked eyes and held hands tightly. Lisa shivered. A fine drizzle had started to fall and the temperature was definitely dropping. But as Rob wrapped his arms around her, she felt warm all over.

CHAPTER THIRTEEN

"Where could they be?" Shanon exclaimed, pacing from one end of the sitting room to the other.

Two whole hours had passed since the Book Talk ended. Outside it was dark and rainy.

"The temperature's dropping," Amy fretted. "I hope they wore coats."

"I hope they took umbrellas," Max said. "Of course they'd look kind of silly carrying umbrellas on bikes," she laughed nervously.

"Of all the silly tricks," Amy grumbled, tossing a pillow down. "Palmer has pulled some doozies in her time, but sneaking off to Ursula Baldwin's for a date—that really takes nerve."

"I can't understand why they didn't tell us," Shanon said, sounding hurt. "Lisa's never lied to me before."

"They probably thought we'd be against it," Max said, peering outside. "I wonder what will happen to them if they're caught?" she said after a short silence.

"They'll be grounded for the rest of the school year," Amy said grimly. "I'm glad I'm not the one who's out there in the dark without even a pass."

"That's not the only thing that's worrying me," Shanon put in, running a hand through her hair. She bit her lip. "If they went to Ursula Baldwin's, I'm sure they did go by bike. Suppose they've been in an accident?"

"Palmer's a great biker, and so is Lisa," Amy assured her, though she, too, was feeling concerned.

"They probably stayed inside the house when it started to rain," Max reasoned.

The three friends looked at one another.

"Do you think they stayed in the house with Rob and Greg?" Shanon asked timidly.

Amy's eyes widened. "Maybe they're going to stay there all night!"

"With boys?" gasped Max.

Shanon felt a sinking feeling in her chest. Ever since the beginning of school, Lisa had been heading for trouble. And she'd been so desperate to see Rob. "I hope Lisa knows what she's doing," she said, swallowing hard. "I hope she and Rob aren't . . . well, you know."

Amy nodded knowingly. "I know."

"Gee," Max breathed, "I hope they aren't either."

"Well, whatever happens," said Amy, "I'm not covering up for them."

"I guess we shouldn't," Shanon said. "We'd only get into trouble ourselves."

"I don't want to get kicked out of school," Max said, nodding in agreement. "If Lisa and Palmer want to get into trouble, that's their business."

A sudden knock on the door of the suite startled all three girls. Shanon dashed over to open the door. Maggie stood there in her raincoat.

"Is Lisa here?" she asked.

"Why do you want to know?" Amy blurted out.

Maggie stared at her quizzically. "I haven't seen her since this morning," she said. "We had a little talk yesterday," she told the girls, "and I'm afraid I was a bit harsh with her."

"She's in the bathroom," Max said quickly. "Washing her hair."

Shanon and Amy nodded.

Maggie looked thoughtful. "Dan and I are off to the movies," she said. "It might be the last chance for us to go out before the baby arrives," she added with a smile. "Next week Dan has that conference in Philadelphia. If there are any problems while we're gone, have Kate check with Miss Dewar over in Cabot. She's covering for us."

"Don't worry," Shanon said. "We'll take care of things."

Maggie smiled. "I've always been able to count on you girls," she said. "Where's Palmer, by the way?" she added.

"In her room, asleep," Amy said, looking away.

Maggie turned toward the door. "Sweet dreams. Don't tell anybody," she said with a wink, "but you girls have always been my favorites! Sorry you didn't get that big room you wanted."

"Thanks, Maggie," Amy said guiltily. "Maybe next year."

Max, Amy, and Shanon all drew big sighs of relief when Maggie finally left the suite.

"That was close," said Amy.

Max nodded. "I think she believed us."

"And we just said we weren't going to cover up for Lisa and Palmer," Shanon said, wincing. "We must have told a hundred lies in the course of five minutes," she murmured. She looked at Max. "What made you say Lisa was in the bathroom?"

"Somebody had to think of something," Max said staunchly. "Lisa is our—I mean your—friend, and Palmer's our suitemate."

"You're right," said Amy. "We couldn't let them get into trouble."

Shanon crossed to the window. Outside it was still raining, the wind howling louder than ever. "At least they have time to get back while Maggie and Dan are gone," she said. "They won't get caught sneaking back into the dorm."

"If they decide to come back tonight," Amy said meaningfully.

"It would be a big mistake to stay all night at Ursula Baldwin's house with a bunch of boys," Max said, shaking her head. "Who knows? Some neighbor might see a light. And if Palmer couldn't explain that she was a friend of Ursula's, all four of them might get arrested."

"Heavy," Amy said dramatically. "Then Lisa and Palmer would definitely get kicked out of school. They could go to jail for trespassing. And so could Rob and Greg Proudfoot."

"That does it!" Shanon said suddenly. "Let's go!"

"Where?" Amy asked in amazement.

"We can't let Lisa and Palmer ruin their whole lives," she said. "If they're so stupid that they make the wrong choices, we have to make the right choices for them."

"You mean we should go get them?" Max asked.

"That's exactly what I mean," said Shanon. "Lisa McGreevy is my best friend, and I'm not going to let her destroy her entire school career."

Within two minutes, the girls were out in the yard. Dressed in slickers and boots, they quietly pulled out their bikes.

"Maggie and Dan have already left," Shanon whispered, noticing that their parking spot was empty."

"I brought a poncho for Palmer," Amy announced, climbing onto her bike.

"Great," Max hissed. "I went to Lisa's room and got her raincoat."

Shanon led the threesome down the side of the driveway. They squished through the grass to avoid the noise of the gravel.

"I hope we find them," Amy said quietly.

"Don't worry." Shanon tried to sound confident. "We will."

Once they were outside the gate, the girls sped along rapidly. Amy had brought a big flashlight.

"How much farther to Ursula Baldwin's?" Max yelled from behind.

"About fifteen minutes," Amy replied from the lead. "At the bottom of the hill, just take a left."

"Hey! I see somebody!" Shanon cried out. "Look—there are two people walking up the road."

"It's Palmer and Lisa!" yelled Amy.

Shanon, Max, and Amy sped down the hill. Drenched to the bone, Lisa and Palmer were walking up with their bicycles.

"Are we glad to see you!" Shanon cried, jumping off her bike.

"I'm glad to see you, too!" Lisa exclaimed, giving Shanon a hug. Lisa was so cold she was shivering.

"I've got a raincoat for you," Max volunteered, pulling out Lisa's coat.

Lisa smiled gratefully. "Terrific."

"And here's your poncho," Amy said to Palmer.

"Thanks," Palmer said through chattering teeth. "This

afternoon was so warm, and now I'm freezing."

The group stood huddled in the road, while Palmer and Lisa put on their raingear.

"How come you're on foot?" Amy asked.

"I got a flat," Palmer moaned.

"We were really worried about you," Shanon told Lisa.

"Do Maggie and Dan know we're gone?" Lisa asked nervously.

"Not yet," Shanon said. "Max covered up."

Lisa turned to Max in surprise. "You covered up for us?"

"Amy and Shanon did, too," Max said. "If Maggie asks what you were doing earlier this evening, you were washing your hair and Palmer went to bed early."

Lisa smiled. "Thanks," she said. "We had such a close call at Ursula Baldwin's," she said breathlessly. "There was a spot on the rug that we couldn't get out."

"On the rug?" Amy said. "You went inside?"

"It's a long story," said Lisa, "but we broke something, too, or rather Greg did. Rob wanted to stay longer, but of course I got really nervous because I kept thinking of the caretaker."

"Caretaker?" Max asked in bewilderment.

"There must have been one," Palmer explained, "because the pool was covered."

"I hate to interrupt this exciting saga," Amy said urgently, "but we'd better hit the road. Someone might miss us if we're gone too long."

The girls ran up the road with their bikes, a hard cold rain beating down on them.

"We're home free," Amy said, seeing the school lights just up ahead.

"Not quite," gasped Shanon. Behind them flashed the lights of a car.

"My gosh," Lisa breathed, seeing the old sedan pull up to the gate. "That's Maggie and Dan's car."

"It couldn't be," Amy stammered in confusion. "They went to the movies."

The girls walked the last few feet to the entrance. The car had stopped just in front and whoever was inside had shut off the engine. In the light of Amy's flashlight, they could make out Dan Griffith walking toward them.

"What's the meaning of this?" the teacher asked sternly.

"You were supposed to be at the movies," Amy blurted out in confusion.

"We didn't like the movie," Dan snapped, "so we left. And I must say I don't like this either," he added. "Why are the five of you off campus without permission in the middle of the night?"

"But it's not the middle of the night," Lisa said, breathing heavily. "It's still early—it's just dark. And we're only outside the gate. Anyway, I can explain everything," she said, "or I think I can—"

"We were just exercising," Palmer broke in.

"Exercising?" Dan said in a booming voice. He walked over to Palmer and stared down at her.

"We decided to go for a bike ride," Palmer continued stubbornly. "There's no rule against bike riding."

Maggie got out of the car and joined the group. "I'm surprised at you girls," she said sadly. "What on earth could prompt you to be out on the road at this hour, especially in this kind of weather? It isn't safe."

"Let's not stand here in the rain," Dan said sternly. "Into the dorm."

"What are you going to do to us?" Lisa asked as the girls hurried up the road.

"On Bounds," Dan said grimly.

Amy gasped. "On Bounds?"

"You know what that means," Dan said. "Grounded for a month with full work detail."

"For a whole month?" Shanon asked, scarcely able to speak.

"At least a month," Dan replied. "Being off campus without permission is a serious offense. I don't care how early it is or how much you like bicycling."

The group trooped meekly inside the front gate and made their way in silence to the dorm.

"Thanks a lot, Palmer," Amy said sarcastically as soon as the girls were back in Suite 3-D.

"Thanks for what?" Palmer squeaked guiltily.

Amy glared. "For telling Dan that *we* were out exercising!"

"I couldn't tell him where we *really* were!" Palmer hissed. "If my mother ever found out I went to Ursula Baldwin's house and brought my friends without even asking, I'd be in a lot more trouble than this."

"That's your problem, not ours," Max muttered, fixing her gaze on the floor.

Shanon sighed. "We won't be able to go to the dance marathon, or leave the school for weeks and weeks."

"We're going to have to spend all our free time working," Amy grumbled.

"I . . . I'm sorry," Lisa offered, touching Shanon's elbow.

Shanon shook Lisa's hand off and walked toward her room. Max followed and shut the door behind her.

"Well, good night, I guess," Palmer mumbled, slinking off to her bedroom. "Are you coming?" she asked Amy meekly.

"I don't even want to sleep in the same room with you," Amy said coldly. She stalked ahead of Palmer and grabbed a blanket. "I'm going to sleep by myself in the sitting room!"

"I'd better be going then," Lisa said, backing out of the door. "Guess I really blew it," she said to Amy.

"You and Palmer blew it, all right," Amy said, slamming the door.

Alone in the corridor, Lisa stared at the closed door of her old suite and started to cry.

CHAPTER FOURTEEN

Dear Nikos,

Lisa and Palmer's nifty party turned out to be a bummer for all us Foxes. Even though the faculty doesn't know the details, we all got punished for being outside the gate past dark without permission. This is kind of a serious offense. So—sorry, but I won't be able to dance my legs off with you at the Ardsley dance marathon. I am really mad!

> *Catch you when I'm out on parole,*
> *Amy*

Dear Mars,

I have not felt this miserable in a long time. I'm in big trouble and can't go to the dance. Thank you for coming to the Book Talk. I thought your comments about Watership Down *were very intelligent. The first issue of* The Ledger *came out and it looks great. But even that does not make me happy. I am sick at heart knowing that an op-*

portunity to see you at the dance marathon is coming up and I can't take it.

Sorrowfully,
Shanon

Dear Holbrook,

Maybe you figured out that the person who wanted to know all about Greg Proudfoot was me. You were right about Greg Proudfoot—he is a real dork! Now I think I would probably say yes to your invitation to the dance marathon, except that I can't go at all because I'm grounded. I was trying to do a favor for one of my friends, Lisa McGreevy, and then got a flat tire and got into trouble. I can't say anything more than that. Hope your chess is going well.

Sincerely,
Palmer

Dear Paul,

I can't go to the dance with you because I am On Bounds. All five of the Foxes are being punished. The day we saw you at the Book Talk, Amy, Shanon, and I went to rescue Lisa and Palmer and then all of us were caught outside the gate. By the way, don't ever tell anybody else about the pool party because it turns out that Palmer did not even know the person whose house she invited Lisa, Rob, and Greg to. How are you? I am terrible. I have been spending hours and hours raking leaves as part of the work detail of my punishment. Palmer has to clean bathrooms, which I think is only fair since she's mainly to blame for all this. Lisa and Amy have to work in the mail room and Shanon has to repair books at the library. And all with no social life—it's the pits!

Sincerely,
Maxie

Dear Rob,

Our time together was wonderful, but unfortunately I am upset. Please tell me, Rob—why did you tell the other guys about the party Palmer and I were giving? I know that you thought telling your closest friends would be okay. Actually, I should have told my closest friend (Shanon) the truth myself. But if Shanon, Amy, and Maxie hadn't known about Palmer and me being with you and Greg at the pool party, maybe they would not have gotten into trouble. You see, when Palmer and I didn't come back right away (we had to fix the house up before we left), they came after us. Then all five of us got caught. To make a long story short, all my friends are in trouble because they were worried about us and broke the rules to try and help us. I guess I can't blame you, though. The only one I can blame is myself.

Sorry, but I'll have to miss seeing you at the dance marathon. Keep your fingers crossed that I'm not grounded for too long. The worst thing about what's happened is that Shanon, Amy, and Max are grounded, too, and they're really mad at me.

I feel awful,
Lisa

CHAPTER FIFTEEN

"If it weren't for certain people we'd be at Ardsley Academy tonight," Amy muttered under her breath the night of the dance marathon. Except for the girls in Suite 3-D, Fox Hall seemed deserted.

"You can talk to me directly, Amy," Palmer announced loudly. Her face slathered with cold cream, she flounced across the room and sat on the pink loveseat. "I am so exhausted," she said, propping her feet up on Amy's guitar case. "I never knew it took so much energy to clean toilets."

Amy glared at her. "Hoisting big bags of mail around for Ginger isn't so great either," she said. "And I wouldn't be spending all my free time doing it, if it wasn't for you."

"Don't yell at me," Palmer snapped. "I'm just as bummed out as you are and disappointed about not going to the dance, even though I would have had to go with Holbrook."

"Will you two stop it!" Shanon sighed from the desk. "We're not going to the dance tonight, so what's the point in arguing?"

"Don't tell me you've forgiven Lisa and Palmer for what they did!" exclaimed Amy.

Shanon's shoulders slumped. "I don't think that what Lisa and Palmer did was right," she admitted. "But I'd rather try to get something accomplished than spend the evening fighting," she said, bending over her Latin book.

"How can you work on a night like this?" Max groaned. "When the rest of the world is having fun?"

"It is kind of difficult," Shanon said sadly. "Maybe the best thing we could do is go to bed early."

There was a light tapping on the door, and Max popped up to open it. Lisa stood in the hall, looking sheepish. "I got lonely," she said, but Max had already turned around and was walking back into the room. Amy picked up her guitar and began to strum it tunelessly. Even Shanon ignored her.

"Come on in," Palmer cried eagerly. "It's still three against two, but with you here at least there'll be someone on my side."

Stepping in hesitantly, Lisa slouched against the wall. "Still mad at us?" she asked, glancing at Shanon.

"It's not so much that Palmer's exercising story got us all in trouble," Shanon said quietly; "the thing I can't forget is that you lied. You told me you were going to the language lab."

"We've been through this a billion times," Lisa cried in frustration. "I'm sorry, sorry, sorry! But If I had told you what I was planning to do that day, you would have tried to talk me out of it."

"We certainly would have," Max said.

"That's because you're such goody-goodies!" Palmer huffed.

Amy's mouth dropped open. "After everything that's happened, I can't believe you said that! Do you realize how much trouble you'd be in if we hadn't covered up for you? If Maggie and Dan ever found out the whole truth—"

"If they ever found out the truth, they'd find out that you, Shanon, and Max had broken even more rules!" Palmer interrupted. "Don't forget—you went to Ursula Baldwin's, too."

"You—you said it was okay," Shanon sputtered.

"Even if I did, you told Maggie you were going to the library that day. Besides," she added, tossing her head, "I was only trying to be nice to you guys."

"Nice to us?" Amy sputtered.

"Everybody had a good time using Ursula's pool," Palmer declared. "And Lisa practically begged me to let her and Rob have their date there."

"I did," Lisa admitted, "but I didn't know that you and Ursula Baldwin were total strangers."

"We're not total strangers," Palmer corrected her. "She knows my mother. And if she had met me, she would definitely have invited me over to her house. I know it!"

"What difference does it make now?" Shanon sighed. "It's over. Besides, Amy, Max, and I lied, too. We told Maggie that Lisa and Palmer were in the dorm, when all the while we knew they were out on a double date."

"I was only trying to help them!" Amy insisted. "I may be a lot of things, but I'm not a rat! We covered for Palmer and Lisa because they're our friends and we didn't want them to get into trouble. At least they used to be our friends."

"What a mess," Lisa said hopelessly. She and Shanon traded glances. "I wish I had told you I was going to see

111

Rob," she said with a catch in her throat. "Then maybe you would have talked me out of it. Because this is definitely not worth it."

"Not worth it?" Shanon asked softly.

"It wasn't worth it to see Rob—not if we're all fighting each other," Lisa admitted. "It wasn't worth us not being friends anymore."

A heavy silence hung over the suite as the girls settled down in various corners. Nobody wanted to sit too close to anyone else.

"Can I come in?" A soft knock announced Maggie Grayson-Griffith's arrival. "I thought I'd say 'Hi' since we're the only ones left in the dorm tonight," she said. She gave them a sympathetic smile. "Sorry you're missing the big dance."

"It's okay," Lisa said.

"Would you like to sit down?" Amy invited, motioning toward the loveseat.

"Don't mind if I do," Maggie said, "but I'd better take the armchair." She looked around the room again. "I really am sorry about the dance," she repeated, "but the rules we have about passes are for your own protection."

"We know that," Lisa said quietly.

"Did you have enough to eat for dinner?" Maggie asked.

"I couldn't eat," Palmer said glumly.

"I couldn't either," the teacher volunteered. "I kept feeling something queasy in my stomach. Maybe it was the eggplant Mrs. Butter served for lunch. In any case," she added, "if you want to come down to the apartment later, I have some gingerbread."

"That's nice of you," Lisa said with a gulp. Suddenly she felt so guilty! Palmer had lied about knowing Ursula Bald-

112

win, but it was Lisa who'd gotten them all in trouble. Hadn't she begged and begged Palmer to let her arrange the double date? Ever since the beginning of school, she'd been putting herself and her feelings for Rob before everything. Not only that, she'd been deliberately mean to Max. And now, because of her, *everyone* was being punished!

"Gosh," Maggie murmured suddenly, "there goes that indigestion again."

Lisa rushed to the teacher's side. "I've got something to tell you!" she cried anxiously.

"What is it?" Maggie asked, wiping her brow. "Whew!" she said under her breath. "It's awfully warm in here."

"Do you want us to open the window?" Shanon asked.

"Thanks," Maggie replied. "What is it you want to tell me?" she asked Lisa.

Lisa glanced at the other girls. Maybe if Maggie knew that they had only been trying to cover up for her, their punishment wouldn't be as serious. It seemed so unfair that Amy, Shanon, and Max had to suffer when she and Palmer were the guilty ones.

"There's . . . something that Palmer and I have to talk to you about," Lisa said with her face burning.

Palmer turned pale. "Me?" she squeaked. "*I* don't have anything to say."

"It's about that night you found us on the road," Lisa went on heedlessly. She knelt in front of Maggie and grabbed her hand.

"I don't . . . think . . . I can listen to it right now," Maggie said with a strange expression on her face.

"Did you hear that?" Palmer hissed. "She doesn't want to listen to it!"

"How come?" Lisa asked innocently.

113

Maggie smiled faintly. "Because I think I'm going to have my baby," she said softly.

Lisa's eyes flew open. "A baby?"

"Now?" Shanon asked, darting over.

"What are we going to do?" said Max. "Where's Dan?"

"I'll go get him," Amy offered, dashing toward the door.

"Wait!" Maggie called. "Dan's not here. He's in Philadelphia this weekend." Breathing more easily, the teacher was quiet for a minute.

"How do you feel?" Palmer asked timidly. "Does it hurt?"

"It did a minute ago," Maggie confessed. "But I'm fine now." She made a move to get up from the chair and the girls rushed to her side.

"Don't worry," Lisa said, "we're here. Do you want us to call the hospital?"

"I'll call my doctor in a little while," Maggie said reassuringly. "This could be a false alarm. Or else the beginning of a very long night," she added. "My doctor and midwife both warned me that women usually have a very long labor with their first baby. I may not get another contraction for half an hour. I do think I'll go down to the apartment, though," she said, "so I can be near the telephone."

On her way to the door, Maggie stopped short. This time there was no mistaking the expression on her face. She was obviously in pain.

"Is it happening again?" asked Lisa anxiously.

"It sure is," Maggie said, sounding surprised. "And this time the contraction was much stronger."

With Lisa and Amy supporting her, she sat down in the chair again. "I hope I can remember the breathing tech-

114

niques Dan and I learned in our Lamaze class," she said, looking a little scared. "What time is it?" she asked, taking a deep breath.

"Nine-fifteen," Max announced nervously.

"Write it down," Maggie instructed Max. "That way we can time the contractions."

"Oh, no," Palmer wailed. "You're not going to have the baby here, are you?"

"Don't worry," Maggie said. "I may have to go to the hospital sooner than I thought, though."

"Where's the doctor's telephone number?" asked Lisa, taking charge.

"Downstairs, by the phone," Maggie replied. "There's a number for Dan's hotel in Philadelphia there, too."

"Come with me, Amy," Lisa commanded. "You stay here with Ms. Grayson-Griffith, Shanon."

"I'll time the contractions," Max said.

"What about me?" croaked Palmer.

"Get her a pillow," Lisa said. "Everything's going to be okay, Ms. Grayson-Griffith," she added, darting out the door.

"I'm sure glad you girls were in the dorm tonight," Maggie said appreciatively.

"Me, too," Shanon said, patting her hand as Palmer slipped a pillow behind her back. "Now, try to relax. Lisa's calling the doctor."

Maggie winced as another contraction began. "Oh, no," she groaned. "I'm already having another one."

"Lisa's got the doctor on the line!" Amy yelled up the stairs. "How are the contractions coming?"

"She's having another one!" Max called back.

"They shouldn't be coming so quickly this early," Maggie said, panting hard. "I hope nothing's wrong!"

"The doctor's sending an ambulance," Lisa called from downstairs.

"Do you have your clothes packed?" Palmer asked in a shaky voice. "You can't go to the hospital without anything to wear."

"My suitcase is all packed and in the front closet," Maggie assured her.

"I'll go get it," said Palmer.

Lisa appeared at Maggie's side. "Amy's waiting outside for the ambulance," she reported. "I got Dan on the phone, and he's taking the next flight home. Do you think you can walk?" she asked solicitously.

Maggie pushed herself up with Shanon's help. "Sure I can," she said. "This time tomorrow there'll be a new little 'Fox' in Fox Hall. I hope it's a girl."

With Shanon and Lisa on either side and Max following closely, Maggie made her way down the stairs.

Amy had thrown the front door open. Outside the moon was full. "Quite a night," Amy muttered, gulping in the cold air.

A distant siren announced the ambulance's approach.

"That was quick," Lisa said, helping Maggie on with her coat.

"Do you want us to go with you to the hospital?" Shanon asked gently.

"You girls need your rest," Maggie said. "I can manage on my own. Besides," she said in a half-joking voice, "you're not allowed off campus." A look of pain flashed across her face again and a single tear rolled down her cheek.

"Please let us go with you," Lisa pleaded.

"It would make us feel much better," Shanon said urgently. "Otherwise we'll all just be sitting here and worrying. . . ."

As the ambulance pulled up to the curb, Maggie nodded at Lisa and Shanon.

"How are you feeling?" a medic asked, coming forward.

Maggie smiled. "Like I'm having a baby. Mind if two of my girls ride along?"

The medic and the ambulance driver settled Maggie into the ambulance, and Lisa and Shanon climbed in behind. Palmer followed timidly to hand them the suitcase.

The inky black sky was scattered with stars as white and jagged as icicles. And the flashing light on top of the ambulance made the sidewalk glow eerily.

"Good luck," Amy called, waving.

"Take care," cried Palmer.

"I'll feed Gracie in the morning and take her for a walk," Max promised.

The ambulance pulled away from the curb swiftly, taking Maggie, Lisa, and Shanon to the Brighton hospital. Amy, Max, and Palmer stood alone in the damp darkness until the siren had faded into silence. Then slowly they returned to Fox Hall.

In the back of the ambulance, Maggie lay quietly on a stretcher. Holding hands, Shanon and Lisa watched anxiously as a medic took their teacher's blood pressure.

"Is she okay?" Shanon asked.

"Her blood pressure is up," the medic murmured, "but we're going to take care of her."

"Did you hear that, Maggie?" Lisa said softly. Maggie managed a little smile. "Everything's going to be all right. . . ."

CHAPTER SIXTEEN

"All right, girls," Dan said. "You can come in now."

The five Foxes tiptoed into the quiet hospital room. Everything was so peaceful. It was hard to believe that less than twenty-four hours had passed since Maggie's labor began in Suite 3-D.

"Hi," Maggie said softly. She waved the girls into the room, while Dan stepped aside. In the curve of her arm was a tiny pink bundle swathed in a blanket.

"Come closer," she beckoned. "It's okay."

With Lisa in the lead, the group crept forward. Maggie loosened the blanket gently, so that the baby's face was showing.

"She's so beautiful," breathed Max.

"I'm glad she's a girl," Shanon whispered happily.

Maggie's eyes glistened. "I'm glad she's a girl, too," she said, "though I'm sure I would have loved her just as much if she were a boy."

"Did it hurt?" Palmer asked, sitting down cautiously on the edge of the bed.

Maggie nodded. "It was rather painful," she confided

with a little smile, "but now all I can think of is that Dan and I have a wonderful baby."

She glanced lovingly at her husband across the room. Dan moved in closer.

"I'm sure glad you girls were there to help out," he said. "I could kick myself for going to that conference so near to Maggie's due date."

"Don't worry, Mr. Griffith," Palmer said proudly. "We knew what to do."

"When are you coming home?" Amy asked Maggie.

"Is there anything else we can do for you?" Max chimed in. "I'm already taking care of Gracie."

"Thanks," Maggie said. "I don't know how we'd have managed without you." She smiled as the baby made a tiny gurgle. "It might be time for an early lunch," she announced. "Is it time for lunch?" she asked the baby playfully.

"She's so small," exclaimed Shanon wistfully.

"Would you like to hold her?" asked Maggie.

Shanon held out her arms and took the baby carefully. "Gee, she feels wonderful."

"Did you name her yet?" asked Amy.

Maggie looked hesitant. "Should we try it out on them?" she asked Dan.

"We have a name in mind, but we haven't quite decided," Dan explained.

"What is it?" Lisa asked eagerly.

Dan grinned. "Camille. For short, we would call her Cami."

"Hi, Cami," Shanon crooned to the baby.

"Cami Grayson-Griffith has a nice ring to it," said Lisa.

"Really cute," Palmer approved.

"I thought you didn't like babies," Amy teased her.

Palmer blushed. "I guess I was wrong, because I definitely like this one."

"I think the name is perfect," Lisa volunteered.

Shanon carefully gave the baby back to Maggie.

"What do you think of your new name, Cami?" Maggie cooed to the baby. The baby gurgled and stretched. Maggie chuckled. "I think she likes it, too," she said.

"Come on, girls," Dan said, opening the door quietly. "Maggie and Cami will be home in a couple of days. There'll be plenty of visits then, especially from willing baby-sitters."

" 'Bye," Maggie called with a parting wave. "See you back at Fox Hall."

"Maggie looks okay for someone who just had a baby," Palmer exclaimed once they were outside of the room.

"She looks really happy," observed Lisa.

"We're both ecstatic," Dan said warmly as he walked the girls out to the lobby. "I can't thank you girls enough for taking over the way you did. Maggie's labor was very unusual for a first child. From what the doctor had told us, we expected the labor pains to be very far apart in the beginning."

"Maggie's sure weren't," Max giggled.

"You girls thought—and acted—very quickly," said Dan. "And fortunately things turned out all right for us and the baby. How are you getting home?" he asked, putting an affectionate arm around Lisa's shoulder.

"Miss Pryn is sending the same van she had come pick me and Shanon up from the hospital last night," Lisa answered. "It was nice of her to give us all special permission to visit this morning, even though we're still On Bounds."

"In view of the way you helped out last night," Dan said, "I'm not surprised she did. Of course, I'm not sure I can do much about your being grounded. Though, now that I think about it," he added, "being On Bounds for a whole month is a pretty stiff sentence for just straying a few yards outside the gate without permission. . . ."

Lisa gulped. Maybe if Dan knew the whole story, he'd let Amy, Shanon, and Max out of the punishment. "There's something else you should know," she said.

"What?" asked Dan.

Palmer crept up behind Lisa. "Please, don't—" she whispered.

"I think what Lisa is trying to say is that we're really sorry," Max chimed in, coming forward.

"And we've learned our lesson," Amy volunteered.

"We'll never go bike riding again in the middle of the night without permission," Shanon promised.

"Or do anything else against the rules," Palmer said sincerely.

Dan smiled. "I believe you mean that," he said. "There's your van," he announced, looking out of the window.

The van honked and the girls scrambled outside.

"See you later!" Max called gaily.

"Hold down the fort until we get back!" yelled Dan.

Once they were in the van, Amy, Lisa, Max, Shanon, and Palmer all sat quietly for a moment.

"I was about to confess everything," Lisa finally said, giving Max a significant look. "You covered up for me again. Thanks."

"Next punishment up from On Bounds is suspension from school," Max said. "I wouldn't want that to happen to you and Palmer."

Lisa smiled at her gratefully and so did Palmer. Then Shanon and Amy smiled at each other, too. In spite of everything, they were still friends—all five of them!

Dear Rob,

Friendship is a funny thing. It has its ups and downs. First, I was jealous of Max, but now I like her! And even though Shanon isn't my roommate anymore, she's still my best friend! Things are settling down at school, and even Amy and Palmer are getting along these days.

Maggie and Dan had their new baby! Her name is Cami, and it's really different having her downstairs in the dorm. She cries a lot, but she's adorable. It's going to be fun baby-sitting for her. Shanon, Max, and I are going to do it together. Even Palmer wants to try! It feels so great, now that we're all friends again. I'm glad that you and I are still friends, too. Someday our punishment will be over and maybe I'll be able to see you again. Until then, please keep writing!

Your letters are my life!

Lisa

TODAY'S HER LUCKY DAY—
MAIDA GOT HER NAME
IN A PEN PALS BOOK!

Maida Moncrief from Huber Heights, Ohio, wrote PEN PALS Headquarters and told us about herself and her pen pal Jodi Winchester. Maida and Jodi have a lot in common and hope to meet each other one day. They read the same books and watch the same shows on television. They write each other as often as possible and call each other on birthdays and holidays. Jodi is not only Maida's favorite pen pal—she's Maida's best friend!

Congratulations, Maida! Check out page 65 in book #18, *Double Date*, and you'll find that a character has been given your name. The character named Maida is an Alma Stephens student—a resident of Cabot Hall and very intelligent! Don't thank us, Maida. Thank Sharon Dennis Wyeth for making your name famous!

You can have your very own pen pal, too. All you have to do is fill out the form on the next page and send it in. We want to find you the perfect pen pal ASAP!

People *really do* get Pen Pals! So get into the act—don't let Maida and Jodi have all the fun!

WANTED: BOYS — AND GIRLS —
WHO CAN WRITE !

Join the Pen Pals Exchange and get a pen pal of your own!

Fill out the form below.

Send it with a self-addressed stamped envelope to:

PEN PALS EXCHANGE
c/o The Trumpet Club
PO Box 632
Holmes, PA 19043
U.S.A.

In a couple of weeks you'll receive the name and address of someone who wants to be your pen pal.

Cut here --

PEN PALS EXCHANGE

NAME _____ GRADE _____

ADDRESS _____

TOWN _____ STATE _____ ZIP _____

DON'T FORGET TO INCLUDE A STAMPED ENVELOPE
WITH YOUR NAME AND ADDRESS ON IT!

Please check one
☐ I bought this book in a store.
☐ I bought this book through the Trumpet Book Club.

Look for your name in PEN PALS books. We'll pick names of matched up Pen Pals every month to print right in a PEN PALS book.